The Girl Under the

Printed in the United States of America

First Printing, 2022
Line Editing: Grace Michaeli

Contact: alex@authoralexamit.com
http://authoralexamit.com/

ISBN: 9798416214296

The Girl Under the Flag

Part 2

Alex Amit

A Puppet

End of November, 1943

Secret

11/23/1943

From: Western Front Wehrmacht Command

To: Army Group France

Subject: Preparations for the winter

Background: Russian forces intend to launch a winter offensive in the east.

General: On the Führer's orders, all forces in occupied countries are to supply food from local resources.

Task:

1. Collect food and other supplies to maintain an adequate standard of living for the army units throughout the Paris area.

2. It is the army officers' responsibility to take care of any shortages that may arise from local sources.

SS. Telegram 641

The eighth arrondissement,

the mistress on the fourth floor

"You were perfect this morning, dear, as always," Herr Ernest tells me after a few minutes, as I'm catching my breath. My eyes are fixed on the chandelier hanging on the bedroom ceiling, waiting for him to kiss me once on my cheek before he gets up and goes to his clothes, to get dressed.

"I enjoyed it too." My hand pulls the blanket up to cover myself once I am free of his body weight and can breathe freely. Even though he knows my body, I still make sure to hide my nakedness from his eyes whenever I can.

Whenever he arrives at the apartment, he leaves his uniform carefully folded on the chair by the bed before approaching me. But first, he places his army boots next to the dark wooden legs of the seat, leaving them standing as if they were two black Doberman dogs waiting for their master to return, alertly watching me the whole time we are together.

"I brought you some cans of corned meat."

"Thanks."

"And next time, I'll try to get some coffee. I saw you're out."

"Yes, I'm out."

Despite the cold in the bedroom, Herr Ernest dresses slowly, paying attention to every detail as he stands in front of the mirror hanging on the wall, tucking his shirt into his pants, and examining the medals on his chest.

"Aren't you cold? I'll make sure someone brings you new firewood."

"Thanks, but I'm fine."

"I do not want you to catch a cold."

"Would you like me to make you some coffee?"

"No, I'm in a hurry." He arranges his belt. "The wine you served last night..."

"What about it?"

"Is it the Château Lafite-Rothschild 1934 bottle I brought last week?"

"Is it okay that I opened the bottle? You did not tell me you wanted to keep it."

"No, it's okay, It's an excellent wine. I'll take care of a few more bottles."

"That will be great."

Herr Ernest bends down to put his boots on, and I hurry out of bed, covering my naked body with the pink silk robe I'd received as a gift, bending at his feet on the parquet floor. The tips of his spiked boots accidentally hit my thigh, hurting me for a moment as I help him force his foot into the neatly polished black boots, but I bite my lip. He never means to.

"Thank you, the robe suits you."

"Thank you."

"I booked tickets for the opera in three days. There will be a Wagner concert."

"I love Wagner, I'll enjoy walking together. I've never been to the opera."

He always informs me in advance, so I will have time to prepare for our meetings, making sure not to surprise me. Even when he arrives early in the morning for a quick visit, he usually sends the driver or his assistant to the boulangerie the day before, letting me know so I will be ready for him.

"I want you to buy yourself a dress for the evening." He pulls his black leather wallet out of his military jacket pocket, placing a few banknotes on the mahogany dresser.

"It's for the dress," he smiles at me, "I know you cannot afford to buy something fancy."

"Thanks." I smile back and walk him to the door.

By the entrance, I hold his grey-green coat while he brings the leather briefcase from the study, the room I am not allowed to enter.

"Thank you for an enjoyable evening. We will meet in three days, I will come to pick you up."

And with those words, I help him fasten his coat, button after button, arranging the leather bag strap over his shoulder before he heads out into the cold stairwell. When I hear his steps going down, I imagine the neighbor from the third floor peeking through the peephole of the door, examining Oberst Ernest on his way out. I know she's cursing me.

I keep my ear against the thick wooden door, listening to the sound of his hobnail boots going down the wooden stairs until I hear the noise of the metal door slamming at the entrance to the building. Only then do I allow myself to sit on the cold parquet floor at the entrance and start crying.

Nothing remains as it was after that night in Normandy.

***

The night wind blew through the big window facing the coast of the Black Sea. Despite the sound of his quiet breathing beside me, I couldn't fall asleep in the foreign hotel room that night in Normandy.

I wanted to go out into the cold night and run to the black shore and the frozen waves, to step inside and just disappear, but I couldn't. The barbed wire or the guards would stop me, bring me back into his arms. Slowly I got out of bed and stepped into the luxurious bathroom, closing the door behind me.

"Everything's fine. You did it. You were fine." My lips whispered as I scrubbed my skin as hard as I could, scratching myself painfully with the bath sponge and shivering at the cold of the water. Philip would never forgive me for sleeping with him, but I kept on rubbing myself, unable to stop.

Only when the cold water was too much to suffer did I walk back to his bed, shivering, covering myself with a blanket, trying to fall asleep, and looking out the black windows.

The next morning, the second time was easier. I thought about the flowers I'd drawn in my notebook and concentrated on the rain falling outside, dripping on the window glass, creating small paths of water. I even managed not to hear the sounds he made and to smile at him when it was all over.

Patiently I stayed down until he got up to get dressed, inviting me to breakfast, starting to get organized for the ride back. My gaze followed him as he stood by the window and looked out into the rain, wearing his neat uniform and humming a German song to himself.

"Did you enjoy it?" He was staring at the grey beach outside.

"Yes, very much, thank you."

"Our breakfast is in a quarter of an hour. I do not want to be late. We have another long drive to Paris." And I tried to cover myself in the blanket before collecting my clothes and going to the bedroom.

On the way back to Paris, my head rested on the closed window while I looked outside to the yellow trees and the river, feeling his hand touch my thigh.

"You're quiet."

"I enjoy looking at the river. So peaceful."

"Yes, so peaceful and faithful, you can always count on it, that's the secret of nature's power."

"I like to observe nature."

"I have noticed. Your drawings in the diary I gave you are lovely."

"When did you see my drawings?" The film box, where is it?

"At the hotel this morning, when you were in the bathroom, I allowed myself to open your bag and look at the diary. Is that okay with you?"

"I thought a woman should have some secrets." The film, had he found it hidden in the bag? He was playing with me and would soon ask the driver to stop the vehicle. Would I be able to cross the river by swimming in this cold?

"Are you cold?"

"Yes, a little cold."

"Should I ask the driver to stop for a few minutes?"

"No, I'm fine."

"Let me wrap you in my coat. You will be more comfortable."

I could feel his hand continuing to caress my thighs through his heavy military coat, wrapping around my body. Please don't ask the driver to stop.

"I brought us a bottle of wine, especially for the way back." He instructed the driver to stop on the side, and while the driver arranged the picnic blanket, I walked away from them by the riverbank and looked at the peaceful grey river. How cold was the water?

***

It was already dark outside as we entered Paris, and the almost-deserted streets were illuminated in dim light. The military vehicle stopped at Place de l'Étoile, at the foot of the silent Arc de Triomphe. I watched the policeman back away into the shadows of the monument, keeping a distance from Herr Ernest.

"It was a pleasant trip," Herr Ernest pulled my body to his and kissed me slowly, his hands holding my neck. "We'll meet again soon."

"I apologize for being so quiet on the way back." I took a deep breath in the cold evening air and tried to overcome my headache.

"I will want to see you more often."

"I'll be glad to." The film box? Did he find it?

Standing still, I waited and watched the military vehicle until it disappeared down the boulevard, leaving the smell of burnt gasoline in the air.

In the first alley, I stopped and, looking back carefully, making sure no one is following me, I slipped into a dark corner. My trembling fingers found it difficult to open the bag's metal buckle, slipping again and again as I looked at the entrance to the alley in fear. The diary was in the bag, and my hand dug through the soft fabric of the dirty lingerie, turning it over and over again, my heartbeat calming down only when I felt the metallic touch of the film box.

The pavement stones were hurting my knees as I leaned on the wall and vomited, feeling the sour taste of wine in my mouth.

After a few minutes I could stand again, breathe the cold night air and start walking home. Again I had to lie to Lizette and hide my true identity, I couldn't tell her that I was the French prostitute of Herr Oberst Ernest.

***

A few days later, Herr Oberst Ernest takes me to a fancy café in front of the opera and lets me know he has found me an apartment.

"Thank you for your concern, but I'm getting along with the woman I live with." I look around at all the German officers sitting with their companions. Do they also have their own apartments?

"I want us to have more time together."

"We can meet as much as you like." I must not push too far.

"I want my intimate time with you."

"I would be happy to visit your place." And be the perfect spouse.

"It's not appropriate for my companion to walk through hotel corridors." He ends the conversation.

"Officer's car special secretaries." I hear the soldiers at the boulangerie laughing among themselves, not before checking there is no officer around.

"But the senior officers receive special corridor girls," they sometimes add, smiling at me while waiting for their baguettes, referring to the hotels confiscated by the German army.

"The maids at the hotels have to separate the uniforms and the lingerie." It is the joke they like most.

"Tomorrow, we will go to see the apartment." Herr Ernest signals to the waiter and I sip my coffee in silence, ignoring the German speech and laughter all around in the café. What did I bring upon myself? How would I leave Lizette?

***

I could not say goodbye to Lizette. I could not experience another farewell. For days, I wandered restlessly in the boulangerie, lowering my eyes in front of Simone's judgmental looks, thinking of what I could possibly say after she treated me so warmly. The nightmares return, and I wake sweaty. Until I can't sleep at all anymore, and I run away.

I pack all my clothes in a big bag and leave the house while Lizette is out, leaving her a small farewell note. Carefully I place it under the picture of the dead man in the silver frame on the fireplace, lowering my eyes and unable to watch his. But he continues to follow me with his proud gaze until I close the door behind me.

Why didn't I stay to hug her one last time? Why didn't I wait to hug Philip that time in the basement? What is wrong with me?

"Do you like the apartment?" Oberst Ernest asks as we walk around the abandoned and furnished place, holding the keys and looking at me.

"Who lived here?"

"It belonged to a family that left France," he answers casually, checking the study, "now it belongs to the German nation."

The creaking of the parquet under my feet feels foreign as I follow him into the study.

"Monique," he looks at me, "this will be my study. You will never enter here." And I turn and go out with a downcast look, concentrating on checking the pantry, my fingers examining the wooden boards.

"I'll make sure they clean here." He follows my fingers. "Do not worry about the dust."

I enter the living room and looking around.

"And I will also take care of new paintings instead of the ones that were taken," he adds as he notices my gaze on the bright spots on the walls. Once there were works of art hanging there, but they are gone.

"Do you like the apartment? I think it will suit you."

I have been living in an apartment that suits me for two months now. I usually wait for him in the evenings, and he comes when he can. I can hear the sound of his hobnail boots on the wooden stairs as he comes. A moment later, he

opens the heavy door with the key
he has, and I wait for him by the
entrance, taking his coat.

"I brought you some boxes of meat
and sausages." He hands me the
heavy paper bag.

"Thanks, but there is no need. I
have enough."

"Any cheese left from the last
time?"

"Yes, there is."

"I'd be happy if you serve it
for dinner, with the red wine I
brought."

"Will you stay the night?"

"Yes." He caresses my side with his
hand.

I exist for those times. For those

nights when he falls asleep after he gets off me, lying in bed.

Quietly I roll up the blanket and carefully walk on the wooden floor, searching in the dark for his brown leather bag lying in his study, the room I must never enter. Listening to every noise, I carefully open the bag, feeling like I'm putting my hand into a monster's mouth as I pull out a pile of documents and take them to the bathroom. Behind a closed door, and by candlelight, I read them. Names of army units, dates and movement orders, fortification instructions, and situation assessments. When I finish, I shove them back into place, exactly in the same order, smelling the leather scent of the heavy bag monster lying on the floor, mixed with the scent of fear coming from my sweaty body.

Then I return to bed with quiet steps and lay beside him. But it is difficult for me to get to sleep again, wondering if tomorrow morning Oberst Ernest will discover what I did and put me by the wall for the last time. Only in the morning, after I hear the building's front door slam, do I allow myself to sit on the cold parquet floor by the entrance and hug myself for a few moments.

Since Normandy, Philip has not hugged me again.

***

The basement

"I've been waiting too long for you." Philip leans against the basement wall, wearing his old leather jacket.

"Someone was standing by the steps of the metro entrance, watching the people. I had to wait for a group of women to pass. I didn't want him to start asking me questions."

"We need to change the method; it's starting to get dangerous."

"The method is fine. I just have to be careful. I know how to be careful."

"I worry about you."

But he does not show it anymore.

He just looks at me from a distance, and all I can smell is this damp basement.

"Your hugs never happened," I whisper to myself.

"What did you say?"

"Oberst Ernest is constantly busy fortifying and preparing for the American invasion. They call the barricades 'The Atlantic Wall.'"

"How do you get along with him? And with Simone at the boulangerie?"

"Right now, they estimate the invasion will take place in the next spring. That's what their intelligence claims."

"And where do they think the invasion will take place?"

"They are concentrating on the Pas de Calais area. The shortest distance from Britain. They have moved another armored division there."

"What about Normandy?"

"It gets secondary priority in their army orders."

"And how do you feel? Aren't you taking too many risks?"

"They are transferring less efficient units to Normandy. Some units are comprised of soldiers forcibly recruited from Poland."

"Does that mean they have a shortage of manpower?"

"It does not seem to me that anything will cause a shortage for the Germans. They always can decide to conquer some nation or piece of land."

"Do you have everything you need?"

"Yes, I'm not missing anything. I have a full pantry. Oberst Ernest is taking care of me." Philip takes a step in my direction, but after a moment, he returns to leaning back against the wall, folding his hands. He can't understand me, it is not his job. It's also not his job to hug me, not after what I'm doing with Oberst Ernest.

"Do you remember the photo film you gave me, from Normandy?"

"I've already forgotten about it."

He was so angry with me then, when I returned from Normandy.

"How could you lose the camera? What will I say to Robert? It took so long to convince him. Do you know the efforts I made to convince him?" He'd walked around the basement shouting at the wall, and I'd stood embarrassed in the corner, ashamed of myself and of what I had done with Oberst Ernest.

"I was not careful enough." I'd tried to stop my tears as I handed him the film I had taken out of my coat pocket, my fingers gripping the small metal box nervously. I'd guarded it for days, afraid of the man in the black coat at the stairs to the metro. Would he choose to search my body?

"Take it, it's for you." I'd approached Philip in fear, wanting to apologize, and did not find the words, but he just put the film box in his jacket pocket and walked away from me. Not even slightly touching my fingers, leaving me waiting to feel warm hands, that time after Normandy.

"London loved the material you photographed; they really appreciate what you did."

"I manage to read a telegram."

"They asked me to relay their appreciation."

"The telegram indicates that the Germans are debating how to deal with the invasion." And I explain to him the movement of forces and units as I remember them. He can pass all that information to those anonymous people living in London. I, too, have no identity. I no longer expect him to hug me anymore.

"Is there anything I can do for you? Can I take care of something for you?" I look at his simple clothes.

"No, thanks. Herr Ernest takes care of everything I need." All Philip cares about is the stuff I bring him.

"Do not forget who you are. You are one of us." He's not trying to hug me.

"I do not forget." I'm a French whore that everyone leaves. You will also abandon me in the end. Luckily, I did not fall in love with you.

"I just don't like you mentioning him."

"I belong to him."

"You are one of us." His fingers are playing with the pencil he is holding.

"I need to go. I have an evening gown I need to purchase." My fingers touch the hem of my coat.

"Take care of yourself." I manage to hear his voice behind me as I climb the stairs leading out of the basement to the rainy street, but I do not turn back.

"Take care of yourself," I whisper as I walk down the alley and wipe away my tears, passing a woman in a grey dress and her daughter, both standing in the doorway of their old shop, watching me walk in the rain. I have to hurry. I have a dress to buy.

***

"I need your help," my lips whisper to Anaïs, trying to make sure the receptionist won't hear me.

"She's with me," says Anaïs to the girl behind the mahogany desk, as she pulls me after her to the back rooms of the fashion house, the space that holds all the rolls of fabric standing against the walls.

"How are you? Tell me, how is he?"

"He's polite."

"Is he gentle?"

"Yes, he is very considerate."

"And does he hurt you?"

"No, never. Does your Fritz hurt you?"

"Sometimes, he has a hard time expressing his real feelings, but I know how to take care of myself. I'm a woman."

My fingers gently caress her hand, but she turns her back to me and lights a cigarette for herself, turning again and exhaling the smoke, closing her eyes with pleasure—the smelly grey-bluish smoke lingers between us. "The most important thing is to know how to take care of yourself. No one else will do that for you."

"I know."

"So, to what do I owe the honor of your visit?" She again looks at me, and I'm sorry for not visiting her before, inviting her to a café, sitting and chatting together. Someday I will, I promise myself.

"I need a dress."

"So let's go buy you a dress. I'm just going to get my bag."

"No, I need a dress from here."

"From here?"

"Yes, I need a dress for the opera."

"Are you going to the opera?"

"Yes, Herr Ernest wants me to be his companion for the opera."

Anaïs looks at me, smoking in silence. Suddenly, she seems smaller and more vulnerable.

"The dresses here are expensive. Do you have enough money?"

"Herr Ernest gave it to me." I put the rolled bundle of bills in her hands, asking anxiously: "Will that be enough?"

"Yes, that will be enough." She slowly examines the bills, returns them to me, and puts out her cigarette. "Not only does Anaïs know how to take care of Anaïs, Monique also knows how to take care of Monique. Follow me."

***

"Anaïs, come here, please," the fashion house manager calls her from the back room. She apologizes to me, asking me to wait a moment.

While standing in the center of the fitting room, I try not to look down at the seamstress kneeling at my feet. They have arranged the red dress wrapped around my body, examined the straps, making sure they do not fall when I bend over.

"Anaïs, please help the lady in the red dress."

The windows of the measurement hall are covered with dark curtains. They probably do not want to stand out in front of the poor city outside.

"Anaïs, please bring the lady a pair of high heels to match the dress, the closed shoes from the winter collection, what is your size?"

There is a stack of wooden chairs in the corner of the room, placed on top of each other. When German women arrive, do they sit comfortably and watch the entire collection? I mustn't look down.

"Anaïs, please arrange the hem for the lady."

"I think it's okay." If only I could run away from here.

"No, we need it to be at the perfect height, Anaïs, please fix that."

Maybe they cover the windows because of the nighttime regulations against bombers? No, they surely don't want to show off.

"This dress looks perfect on you. You're perfect. Thank you, Anaïs, you can go back to the sewing room."

"When do you need the dress?"

"The concert is tomorrow." My eyes follow Anaïs' back, watching her disappear into the back room, closing the door behind her with a slight click.

"Excellent, our courier will

bring you the dress tomorrow morning, give the address to the receptionist."

On the way out, I want to go and say goodbye to her, but the salon manager accompanies me to the exit, kisses both of my cheeks goodbye, and I'm too ashamed to go back.

One day I will visit her, and we will both go for a walk in the street, passing the fancy café and watching the opera house. Tomorrow I will enter it for the first time in my life.

***

Pompeii

"Did you get wet?" Herr Ernest
asks when we get out of the
car, hurrying up the marble
stairs leading to the magnificent
entrance.

"No." But Herr Ernest turns to scold
the boy holding a large umbrella,
and opens the arriving car's doors.

"It's okay."

"No, it's not okay. He needs to
know how to do his job." Herr
Ernest goes down the stairs and
speaks to him in his quiet voice,
and I turning away, looking up at
the big red flags with swastikas
in their center. They hang at the
building entrance, drizzling rain
onto those coming to the concert.

"Shall we go inside?" His hand holds mine. "Be careful not to slip on the wet marble stairs."

At the entrance to the hall, I stop in place, overwhelmed by the golden wealth surrounding me. The crystal chandeliers illuminate the spectacular ceiling paintings and shiny gold sculptures, as if there are no power outages throughout the city. Waiters in black suits and bow ties move quietly among the guests, holding silver trays with champagne glasses. The war did not cross the threshold of the opera, except for the guests, German army officers in pressed uniforms with various ranks and decorations.

"Please, for you." Herr Ernest hands me a clear yellowish glass with small bubbles while bringing his lips closer to my ear, so as not to shout in the bustle of noise all around us: "What do you think?"

"Wonderful." I want to run out of this place, feeling so prominent in my red gown.

"The dress suits you so well." He holds my arm, like all the other German officers traveling in the hall in their uniforms, proudly presenting their female companions wearing their prom dresses, as if they were a valuable prize.

"Come, I will introduce you to some of my colleagues." He leads me to the center, under the huge golden chandelier.

"And how come a young French lady like you is interested in Wagner?" A senior officer in a black uniform and visored hat turns to me in French, looking at me mockingly.

"There are young ladies who love his music and his opinions," I answer in perfect German, looking at the skull decorating his hat.

"You did not tell us she speaks German." The officer turns to Oberst Ernest while appreciatively looking at me, and everyone laughs.

"Be careful. Maybe she is a spy." Another officer answers him, his helmet also decorated with a skull, and the sounds of laughter increase.

"It's clear to me she's a spy." Oberst Ernest smiles at him. "Therefore I will keep her close to me, so you can't snatch her. You all know the German rules. What we hunt belongs to us."

"Never trust French women unless they are accompanied by a German officer supervising them," I answer the officer in the black uniform in my perfect German, smiling a perfect smile with my red lips, but my stomach hurts from tension.

"To the beautiful and loyal French women." The officer in black raises his glass in my honor, and I feel the hand of Oberst Ernest tightening around my arm.

"To the thousand-year Reich." Another officer raises his champagne glass, and we all cheer.

"And to the pleasures of Paris," adds another officer.

"And to staying here forever, to never be sent to the Russian front."

"You can trust the Americans who are preparing for the invasion. They will keep us here." The sounds of laughter continue, though no one dares raise his glass.

"To our Führer."

"To the Führer."

"Where are you going?"

"To the ladies' room."

"Hurry up. The concert is starting soon." He releases my arm, and I cross the hall slowly, having a hard time walking on luxurious high heels while knowing that all the officers' eyes are fixed on my back, examining me.

"Are you okay?" she asks me in French as I wash my face in the luxurious restroom.

"Yes, thank you, I was nauseous for a moment."

"It's the champagne. You're probably not used to it."

"Yes, it must be champagne."

I hear the bell ringing in the hall, calling everyone to enter the concert. Oberst Ernest is waiting for me in the emptying lobby, and I watch the column of men holding their colorful wives. They slowly climb up the marble stairs, and I think of the man from the railway company, that time in Drancy, when he told me about the rows of people climbing into the train carriages.

"Are you enjoying the evening?"

"It's a wonderful evening. Thank you for taking me."

When he stays the night in my apartment after being inside me, I sit quietly in the bathroom and read military orders. The Russian winter offensive has begun. Therefore the Final Solution to the Jewish Question must be accelerated.

***

"What is the Final Solution to the Jewish Question?"

"I don't know. How are you? How do you feel?" Philip tries to get closer to me, but I walk backwards until the basement wall's rough stones stop me.

"Check with your Communist friends about the Final Solution."

"They are not just my friends; they are your friends too. If they were not, you would not be here." He keeps his distance. When will he get tired of me?

"The Germans are losing on the Russian front; they've taken huge casualties, whole units have been dissolved."

"I'll give them that; how are you?"

I do not want to tell him how I am. It won't change anything anyway.

"Here in Paris, they are afraid they will be transferred to the East. They are talking about it amongst themselves."

"And what are your feelings, and how is their morale?"

"Their morale is still high,

especially here in Paris where they enjoy all the pleasures of the city, holding French women like me in their arms."

"You are different, you are not like them; you don't have to think of yourself like that."

"I know I'm different from them." Really? What's the difference? That I'm telling you what I read at night? Believe me, I'm licking German boots just like Anaïs and Violette. They at least believe it will help them.

"You are one of us, important and precious."

"I'm aware of that." One of you? One of the resistance? One of the Communists? One who betrays her dead girlfriend? One that everyone abandons in the end? I will stop being one of you as soon as it does not suit you. I know exactly how precious I am.

"I'm worried about you. You're taking too many risks."

"I can take care of myself. Please check with your Russian friends about what I asked, this matter of the Final Solution to the Jewish Question. I have to go."

"Monique, wait." He calls after me, but he no longer chases and hugs me on the stairs. He too has got used to the cold.

On the narrow street where old crates are thrown on their sides, I go to the shop entrance on the other side of the alley, take out a sausage packed in a paper bag and serve it to the small dirty girl who always stands in the doorway, looking at me. She snatches the bag and runs inside the dim shop, disappearing from my sight.

I have learned not to cry.

***

"Darling, what do you want to do this morning?" Herr Ernest asks me a few days later after he gets off my body, and I cover myself, wiping away a tear with the tip of the blanket.

"What were you thinking of doing?"

On Sundays he tends to stay with me until later, looking for something to do for himself and his companion whore.

"Maybe we can go see some art?"

As we go down the building's stairs, passing the third floor, I hear a rustle from the neighbor's apartment door. She peeks at me from the peephole every time I go downstairs. Once, I asked her who owned the apartment I live in, but she refused to tell me and just looked at me with hatred in her eyes, slamming her apartment door in my face.

"Put on your coat. It is cold outside." Herr Ernest holds the front door for me.

In the grey street, his driver faithfully waits for us in the military vehicle, and I wonder if he sat like that all night inside the frozen car.

"Good morning," Oberst Ernest greets him as the engine chokes from an effort to start at low temperatures. "Please take us to the Tuileries Gardens."

"I thought we were going to the Louvre."

"The Louvre is almost empty. The ungrateful French managed to hide away all the paintings. We don't know where."

"I thought you knew everything."

"We Germans have the patience to discover everything about traitors like them." He smiles at me. "And you are one of us, you were born in Strasbourg, remember?"

"I remember."

"I'm happy you are not like them." He puts his gloved hand on my thigh. "You're like us." And I look out the car window and think he is right. I'm like them. I eat German food, warming myself in the cold winter with firewood his driver brings me, and I'm being driven in a German military vehicle on a Sunday morning, watching the almost-empty streets.

"Can you bring more candles the next time you come over?" Power outages have intensified recently, causing a shortage of candles.

"Already finished? I thought there were enough." Even Simone allows herself to smile at me more often, occasionally asking if I can bring her some.

"I used them up."

"Yes, I'll bring you some. Is anything else missing? Stop the car here by the plaza," he instructs the driver.

"No, nothing more."

"Wait for us here, please," he instructs the driver as he opens the car door for me near the entrance to the Tuileries Gardens. Several other military vehicles like ours are already parked next to ours. What exhibition is this?

"This way." Herr Ernest hurries to wrap me in my thick fur coat.

The only sound I can hear as we pass through the gardens' large gate is the gravel under my leather boots, the ones he bought me. The wooden sign is still hanging by the entrance, but I'm not stopping anymore, just looking at the white letters beginning to peel, revealing a rotting wooden board beneath.

"Here." He holds my arm and

points to a hall in the corner of the garden.

A couple is approaching ahead of us, holding a wrapped package, and while the officers salute each other with 'Heil Hitler,' we, the mistresses, examine each other's coats with embarrassed smiles.

"What's this place?"

"It's time to keep my promise."

"What promise?"

The guard at the entrance to the hall salutes and taps his heels, but I am used to it and no longer get tense, just smiling at him politely, hurrying to escape from the cold wind outside, into the hall full of framed paintings.

"What exhibition is this?" I look around. There are thousands of paintings hanging on the walls, in piles on top of each other, or just standing in simple wooden crates in the center of the hall. "Who do these belong to?"

"We came to purchase some paintings," Herr Ernest addresses the older man who approaches us, nodding politely and turning to me.

"What style does the madame like? Or maybe the gentleman decides?"

"The madame decides at home," Herr Ernest smiles and does not scold him. "What style do you like?"

"What is this here? Who do all these paintings belong to?"

"This is a painting store," Herr

Ernest answers me. Like us, several German officers walk around, some with their spouses, some with an assistant who follows them, holding open notebooks and writing down the names of paintings they point at.

"And the price, how much does it cost?"

The older man takes a few steps aside out of politeness, patiently waiting for us to finish the discussion and decide on the style I like.

"These are paintings for sale at an excellent price," Herr Ernest is staring at me with a blank look.

"Who sells these paintings here?" I lower my eyes, but I can't hold myself back. I should be quiet.

"These collections belong to families who wanted to get rid of them, or did not need them anymore, so they sold them, this is a real opportunity. I promised you I would buy you some paintings for your apartment, and I keep my promises." He smiles at me. "What style of art do you like?" He signals to the older man in the suit that the discussion between us is over, and orders him to come close again.

"What would the madame like me to show her?"

"I have to see myself," I answer him hesitantly.

At first, I walk step by step between the paintings, quietly examining the richness that lies before me, raising my eyes and looking at the walls around me, or lowering them and watching the piles that lie on the floor. But then I start to hurry, going through the paintings, checking them one by one, and removing pile after pile while the older man in the suit helps me examine the ones at the bottom, box after box. He is gasping from the effort but keeps calm, and all that time, Herr Oberst Ernest accompanies us in silence, patient with my crazy behavior.

"I want that one," I finally point to a drawing of a smiling dancer, raising her arms high above her head.

"I can see madame loves modern art. You have good taste," the older man compliments me and turns to Herr Ernest for his approval. "It's a painting by a well-known painter."

It seems to me that Herr Ernest is not happy with my selection, but I insist, and he approves with a nod of his head, signaling to a young man standing aside to come take the painting for payment and packaging.

"Is that all you want?"

"Yes, that's all I want, now it's your turn."

Herr Ernest walks slowly, pointing with his finger at the old man to follow him, and chooses a large drawing of a horse race and a painting of hunters hunting a fox in the woods. "It will be perfect for the living room and my study," he explains when the man in the suit marks the paintings for packaging.

As we go out to the car, followed by two employees carrying the paintings we purchased and keeping a respectful distance behind, I give Herr Ernest a hand and thank him for the new purchases.

"You're welcome, my dear. It will make your apartment more pleasant."

The driver standing next to the grey vehicle hurries to open the door, and I wait outside in the chill wind for the store workers to put the packaged paintings in the car.

"Be careful," I ask them, not before looking one last time at the garden gate and the peeling sign. I'm so glad I did not find the painting that hung in my bedroom.

Mom and Dad had given it to me for my tenth birthday. A dancer bending forward, tying her ballet shoes. I'd once wanted to be a ballet dancer very much.

***

The nightclub dancers raise their legs high in the air, stomping to the beat of the loud music, and I watch them through the cigarette smoke that fills the crowded place, trying to look in another direction.

"Try it. You'll love it," Anaïs yells as she brings her lips close to my ears, trying to overcome the noise of the band playing and the crowd loudly talking around us.

"Herr Ernest will not be pleased with that," I answer as I lean towards her, looking through the smoke at the line of dancers on the stage.

"What will he not like?" Violette joins, grimacing as Anaïs points to the pack of cigarettes lying on the table.

"Everyone should have at least one obscene habit," Anaïs laughs, "it will make you feel good, try."

"They say it will soon be impossible to get cigarettes," Violette is almost shouting to overcome the noise.

"It will always be possible to get cigarettes. You just have to know the right way to get them," Anaïs leans back and lights another one for herself. "For what purpose were soldiers invented?"

Oberst Ernest and the two Fritzes sit on the other side of the table, bending towards each other with their backs on us, looking at the dancers and talking, maybe about the war.

"I don't think they're talking about your cigarette stock right now." I laugh with Anaïs.

"They surely are not. They are wondering how high the dancers will lift their legs, and how much they will be able to see." She points with her eyes to the black garters that occasionally flash under the fabric of their dresses.

"It's disgusting."

"You have to get used to it. That's how it is with men. They can sit with you, reading poetry and talking about art and culture, but when they are alone, they go to peep shows in Pigalle."

"Do you think they go to strip shows in those clubs?"

"Even though you were taken to the opera, you remain a little innocent, aren't you?" She blows the cigarette smoke into the dark hall and smiles.

"I think they are talking about the situation in Russia," I try to change the subject and shout in her ear, even though I do not believe it. For a while now, Oberst Ernest has not been talking about the great victories in the East. The rumors about the success of the Russian winter offensive have reached the city's grocery stores, giving the people standing in the endless lines something to gossip about. Even the few people walking on the streets, curled up in their coats, believe that the Germans are in retreat.

"Do they talk about Russia?" asks Violette.

"Yes, but he says we have nothing to worry here in Paris." I answer.

"I want to experience the culture of this city," Herr Ernest pulls me outside almost every evening he comes. "We must be strong against false rumors," he adds as we drive through the cold, dark streets.

The cafés are still full of soldiers, even though some are not heated, and I have to sit wrapped in the fur coat Herr Ernest bought me, looking back at the people outside when they watch me. What does it matter if they spit on the sidewalk? It is wet from the rain anyway.

The telegrams I read at night about the eastern front tell of crushed German armored columns

on the sides of roads and frozen
soldiers dead in the snow. Even
the French-language German army
newspaper, still sold at a stall
on the boulevard, has stopped
reporting on the German army's
strength, concentrating on articles
about fighting spirit in battle.

"I promise you they are not talking
about Russia unless the dancer in
front of them was born in Moscow,"
Anaïs approaches as if whispering
a secret. "Maybe they want to
start practicing their Russian." She
bursts out laughing, looking at us
dismissively.

"What will happen? I'm scared of
the Communists," Violette asks,
not smiling tonight at all.

"What are you afraid of?"

"Fritz treats me so nicely, I'm

afraid they'll send him to the east," she approaches us and tries to whisper, though her whisper sounds more like weeping. "I heard terrible things are happening there."

"They will not send him to the East," I place my hand on hers, trying to calm her down, "they need him here in France."

"I'm afraid it will end one day."

"It will not end," Anaïs answers her, and smiles at me as she puts out her cigarette in the ashtray. "We were promised a thousand-year Reich, weren't we?"

"Sorry, we neglected you." Fritz hugs his Violette, who clings to him tightly, putting her head on his shoulder and looking at us with a smile.

"We thought you were more interested in the dancers," Anaïs answers him, making us laugh.

"Are you going to strip shows?" I bring my lips to Herr Ernest's ear and ask him, trying to be quiet, but he just smiles at me and doesn't answer. Why does Anaïs know such things that I don't? Are all men like that? Does Philip also go to such clubs in the Latin Quarter, ending the night in the bed of a sweaty cabaret dancer? What does it matter at all?

"I want to try," I shout across the table and reach for the cigarette box placed between us. The music bothers me, and in my eyes, the dancers are ugly.

"It's not for you," laughs Anaïs, snatching the box away, "it's just for simple women like me."

"Give her a try. I'll get you more," her Fritz says, but one look at Herr Oberst Ernest silences him, and he places his hand on Anaïs' arm, turning her towards him and kissing her passionately while she strokes his fair hair with her fingers.

"To Paris." I lift my glass of champagne, covering the insult, and everyone joins.

"To German-French friendship."

"To the thousand-year Reich," Anaïs raises her hand, and we all drink again.

"Pour me more," I shout at Ernest. Trying to overcome the noise of the band and the dancers' footsteps in their black garters. At least he allows me to drink.

If I drink a little more, I may be able to stop all my fears and feelings of shame.

***

"Shall I stop?"

"No, it's okay, you can go on."

I can hear the roar of American bombers in the distance. The German searchlights are probably traveling through the dark sky, looking to aim their anti-aircraft cannon batteries and hunt down bombers.

"Does it feel good?"

"Yes, don't stop."

I'm sprawled on the bed with an awful headache. I drank too much tonight.

The whimper of the alarms sounds every few minutes, and the roar doesn't stop, like a muffled gurgle that shakes the window and the parquet floor, causing the iron bed to creak with a shrill sound. But perhaps these are all the movements of Herr Ernest lying on top of me while I close my eyes.

"They are looking for Renault's factories in the suburbs. They will pass us," he whispers hatefully as he continues to shake the bed, and I groan, thinking of the pain that awaits an anonymous young woman now soldering metal plate for a German truck on Renault's production line, somewhere in the suburbs. She doesn't know that in a few minutes, her fate will be sealed. Which of us will hurt more?

"Don't stop." It doesn't matter; death will come for both of us, sooner or later.

***

"Mademoiselle." They approach me the next day on the street, near the opera square.

"I'm in a hurry to the metro, he'll stop working soon, and I have to buy Christmas presents."

"Do not worry about the metro," the tallest smiles, "what do you have in the bag?" And I want to scream.

"I have nothing in the bag." I hand them my ID card with shaking hands, also because of the cold.

"Monique?" he asks in good French, sifting through the certificate, comparing the picture to my face. They stand close to me, hiding me from the other people on the street with their black leather coats. Those few who take a quick look continue walking, thankful for their good luck. I knew it was coming. It was only a matter of time before they got me.

"Were you born in Strasbourg?"

"Yes."

"Date of birth?"

"Fourteenth of December nineteen twenty-five."

"Where did you live in Strasbourg?"
He compares the details to the
notebook he has taken out of his
pocket. What is written there?
What does he know about me? Is
he just trying to scare me?

"What did you ask?"

"Where did you live in Strasbourg?"
He raises his eyes from the
notebook, looking at me.

"Rue de Barr, I think, I was a little
girl. It was by the river. We went
to the river on Sundays." Never
be too confident in yourself. You
are not a notebook of information
in which everything is precisely
written as it happened. They
always suspect someone who
knows all the answers accurately,
as if memorizing them. Philip told
me that, in the old warehouse

south of town, and I think that was the moment I started to trust him.

"Is it close to the river?" The tall one keeps looking at me while his friend examines my tremors with his hand hidden in his coat pocket. What does he have there?

"I think so. Dad used to carry me on his shoulders. I remember there was a playground next to a slide."

"Are you cold?"

"Yes, I do not have a warm coat like yours." If you feel they are starting to suspect you, show some aggression, but not too much, people who feel guilty do not tend to be aggressive. Philip put me in front of the wall and approached me, role-playing with me, and I smelled his body odor for the first time, mixed with the smell of gun oil and the printing ink from his fingers.

"Do you speak German?" The other man asks me in their language.

"Yes, certainly, from childhood," I answer them in German.

"So why didn't you answer us from the beginning in German?"

"Because you approached me in French."

"And why are you not in Germany, with all those now helping the homeland?"

"I help here, selling delicious food at a boulangerie to soldiers who come tired from the front lines. I know how hard it is for them, especially those who fought the Communist monster that wants to destroy us." If you run out of ideas, invent, Philip briefed me, and I sat fearfully in front of him and thought there was no way I could ever invent anything.

"And what's in your bag?" He takes my bag without asking.

"A notebook. I draw sometimes."

He lets the other man hold my certificate while carefully examining the notebook, flipping through the pages, and reading the titles.

"Do you like Normandy?"

"Yes, very much, but we cannot go there now." Be careful not to slip, providing them a piece of information they may check and verify that you are lying to them, like places you have been to or dates. Make sure you stay as general as you can. Philip remained standing close to me, but since then, because of me, everything was ruined.

The short man gives one last look at the diary before closing it and returning it to me.

"Have a good day, Frau Otin."

"You too."

I start walking away, trying to keep calm without looking back, as if nothing had happened, but after a few steps, he calls me again, and I stop, turning back to him, filling the pain in my stomach.

"Frau Otin?"

"Yes?"

"I enjoy strolling the beaches of Normandy."

"The Strasbourg River of my childhood is more magical."

What do they know about Normandy? Why did he say that?

***

"How are you? Is everything okay?"

"Yes, everything is fine." My trembling hand looks for the pack of cigarettes in my bag.

"How was the road here?"

"Nothing special. The same Gestapo men standing on the steps of the metro, examining the people, it's cold to stand like that in the snow for so many hours."

"I worry about you more every time."

"You do not have to worry about me. I know how to get along." I take the matchbox out of my bag, trying to light a cigarette, but my fingers are shaking, and the match is broken, so is the next one. Philip takes the matchbox out of my hands, and gives me a lit match. I inhale the smoke with a look of relief.

"You started smoking?"

"Yes, such an obscene habit." I blow the smoke up, lean back, and look at him.

"I hope you do not smoke next to Ernest. I don't think he would like a woman smoking. It is not feminine."

Is that what interests him? What Herr Ernest will say?

"I manage Herr Ernest. Don't worry about Herr Ernest. Monique knows how to take care of Monique."

Philip examines me, watching with his dark eyes, searching for what to say. It's cold in the basement, and we're both wrapped up in our coats like we'll soon be out of here. Philip notices my eyes looking at his torn gloves, and he folds his arms, trying to hide them, and I want to take off my new leather gloves, another gift from Oberst Ernest. I inhale again. The heat of the cigarette smoke in my throat provides me some comfort.

"You have changed," he says.

I inhale the cigarette again and look at him. I so want to hug his body and promise him I've stayed the same, me and all my thoughts at night. I want to move this distant table that has been standing between us for so long and rest my head on his shoulder, whispering for him to hug me. But I know it's too late, I'm with Herr Ernest, and he has his resistance and maybe a cabaret girl he shares his nights with, getting into her panties like all men.

"Yeah, I've changed, but we did not come here to talk about me, we came to talk about the Germans and the material I have to tell you, didn't we? So let's start."

And he keeps looking at me in silence as I describe all the information I can remember, sketching out a new defense plan I was able to see one night.

"This is important information. I will pass it on."

"Excellent."

"You're doing a great job."

"Excellent." What am I risking myself for, bringing them all this stuff? Why don't they do something with it? What are they waiting for? For them to catch and torture me? For Herr Oberst Ernest to find out who I am? Why aren't they already invading and winning this war?

"What happened?"

"Nothing happened." I stand up from the small table, lighting another cigarette. Suddenly this basement feels too suffocating for both of us.

"You look angry." Philip gets up

with me, trying to get closer, but I walk away from him, blowing the grey smoke in his direction.

"I'm not angry. I'm doing my job excellently. Even you say that."

"So why are you so distant from me?"

"Because I'm already tired and because you chose."

"What did I choose?"

"To send me to him."

"Because I had no choice."

"So I'm with him, and everything's fine."

"You must go on. There is no other choice." He tries to get closer again, but I don't want him to, feeling the basement wall scratching my back.

"I'm getting along great." The cigarette is tossed on the floor, and I crush it with my shoe. The air here is compressed and damp. "I deliver good information, and you keep me alive, a great deal."

Philip pauses, furiously looking at me. "Do not forget who you are."

But I'm tired of everyone trying to explain to me who I am. I don't know who I am anymore, who I'll be when it's all over, and how it will end. I'm not able to change anything anyway.

"Besides, you can ask your fellow Communists to take down the sign that forbids Jews from entering the Tuileries Gardens. It bothers me on my trips with Oberst Ernest, and there are no Jews left in Paris anymore."

Philip looks at me angrily, and for a moment I think I've gone too far, and he will hit me, but he just balls his fists, approaching me and holding my body, biting my lips tightly and making me stop breathing. His hands grab me as he continues to kiss my lips, trying to spread them with his tongue, and for one moment, I allow him to, no longer able to stop myself.

"Merry Christmas." I push him away from me, scratching his neck with my fingers, and escape, knowing that if I stay another moment, I will never be able to return to my apartment in the Eighth arrondissement.

Tonight Philip will probably go out with his cabaret dancer and leave me alone with Oberst Ernest.

At least I can look for the little girl in the alley, giving her two cans of meat that I kept especially for her, for the new year.

***

The snow that has fallen in the last two days has painted the city white, covering the quiet streets in white shrouds. Only a few people are walking in the cold, leaving deep grey footprints in the snow. But most of them remain in their homes as they try to heat the small apartments with some old newspapers or some firewood purchased on the black market, in exchange for ration slips for flour and oil. Some German army truck crosses the boulevard at a slow pace, leaving black streaks on the road as it melts the snow, but the rest of the vehicles disappeared from the streets months ago. There is no fuel. Even the big market has returned to using traditional wooden carts, harnessed to tired horses.

"Merry Christmas," Simone greets us as we wrap ourselves in coats and huddle near the back door of the boulangerie. She even allows herself a moment of sentimentality and hugs us before we head out into the wet and white streets. I have to hurry home. Herr Ernest has informed me he will be coming today.

My cold fingers dig in my bag, searching for the apartment key when I hear a noise from inside, and I freeze.

Is Oberst Ernest early? Are they waiting for me inside? What should I do?

My feet quickly carry me down the stairs as I run out to the street, almost slipping and falling on the wet marble stairs at the building entrance. Panting in the cold air, I keep running to the street corner, ignoring my footprints left behind in the snow. Where shall I go now?

The street is empty, no black car is waiting to pick me up, and I can't see car tire tracks in the snow on the road. Only my steps seem so visible to anyone who wants to chase after me. What should I do? One woman strolls at a distance, bent over, carrying a bundle of wood or rags on her back. She doesn't seem to be one of them. Could I be wrong? Maybe Herr

Ernest is in the apartment waiting for me. Shall I wait for him to arrive?

The street is getting dark as I stand and rub my palms together, trying to move a little and ignoring an older man passing by. He is probably wondering why a woman is waiting like this on a street corner when it's snowing outside. My feet hurt from the cold, but I try to keep on walking, trying to hide from passing cars that might be looking for me. I can't bear it anymore.

I have nowhere else to go. How much longer will I live in such fear?

Slowly I climb the wooden stairs, carefully open the door, release the key, and hold it between my aching fingers, ready to fight as much as

I can or turn around and escape. The house is warm and cozy.

"Where have you been? You're freezing." He walks over to me, helping me remove my coat. "What took you so long? I sent my driver into the street looking for you. I brought us a Christmas tree to celebrate, like in the homeland. Are you okay? Why are you so quiet?"

"I'm cold." Just taking off my shoes and wet socks, and warming up a little by the fireplace, that's all I want now.

At the end of the living room the tree stands proudly, and Herr Ernest goes around it slowly, placing string lights and silver orbs that twinkle cheerfully. It's nice to watch the fire burning in the fireplace, concentrating on the flames that light up the walls and the hunter painting that Herr Ernest bought, a man shooting a running fox, and Mom lights candles. We all sing Hanukkah songs, laughing at Jacob who can't manage the strange Hebrew words, and I whisper the words quietly because I'm ashamed they'll discover who I am, and Dad is touching my shoulder: "Monique, Monique."

"Monique." Herr Ernest whispers to me, gently touching my shoulders, and my eyes look around, trying to figure out where I am and who this man is with the cropped yellow hair and green eyes. "It seems you fell asleep." He looks at me.

"Did I say something?" I straighten up in an armchair in front of the fireplace.

"No, you just mumbled something strange." He continues to examine me. "Look, I made us a Christmas tree, to feel like home."

"It's beautiful. The most beautiful I've ever had."

"I also brought you a present." He points to the box under the tree.

"I'm so sorry. I did not buy you anything. I thought you would return to your family in Germany." I'm looking for a reason. "Do you have family in Germany?"

"I'm an army man. My home is where my boots are." He walks to the Christmas tree and brings my present. "Merry Christmas."

My fingers gently remove the colored ribbon and peel off the paper, grabbing the cardboard box and opening it.

In horror, I examine the brown leather case inside the box, looking at the black metal box with the golden buttons and lens. My fingernails gently scrape the iron eagle engraved on the camera body, holding a swastika with its claws.

"What is it?" I'm looking at him.

"It's a camera. It's your present, the best on the market thanks to our Führer, a Leica camera."

Even if I wanted to get up and run away, I couldn't. My feet are paralyzed. Why did he buy it for me?

"Why?"

"Because it suits you," he is not smiling at me, "you love to draw, and I thought of giving you a present, you should have thanked me for your present."

"I'm sorry." My legs manage to carry me as I stand and approach him, trying to lift my arms and hug his shoulders. "You just surprised me, and I've never had a camera, what do you do with it? Can you show me?"

And Oberst Ernest relents and sits down in the armchair, begins to explain to me how to hold the camera and how to aim and which buttons to press to shoot or pull out the film.

And all that time, I'm kneeling at his feet on the carpet in the living room, asking questions, and making myself interested while trying to warm myself and looking at his fingers holding the metal box. What does he know about me, and how long will I be able to hide myself?

"Next summer, I'll take a few days off from the army, and we'll drive to the beach, maybe to the south of France, and then you can take a picture of us." He looks at me.

"Please pour me some wine," I ask.

"Will you make us dinner? I brought groceries. They're in the kitchen." He strokes my hair as I kneel on the carpet.

"What did you bring?"

"Some things for the holiday." He continues to stroke my hair. "Too bad you don't have pure German blood."

I look up at him questioningly.

"In order to have a legal spouse, an officer in my position must find a German woman with certificates."

"And what about me?"

"After we win the war, you could come with me to Berlin."

My lips are silent as I rest my head on his knee, thinking what to say that would fit, wondering what he would think of my racial purity.

"Merry Christmas." I kiss his knee, feeling the rough pants on my lips. I have to get up and make dinner, and then I can drink the wine he brought. Tonight he will probably let me drink as much as I want to.

***

"See you tomorrow, and watch out for the snow," Simone says goodbye a few days after the new year, and I'm starting my way to the apartment by foot, blowing on my frozen fingers. The metro is not working.

When will this snow end? Maybe it would have been better for the snow to last forever and paint this grey city white. No one will wrap me in white. I will never wear a white dress. I will not even be like the same French woman I saw a few months ago, who married a German officer in the church of La Madeleine. I'd passed by and glanced at them for a moment. All his fellow officers stood in two straight rows on the steps, creating a passage of applause for them while the hem of her white dress disappeared in the church. Even

Herr Ernest doesn't want me, and if he knew who I was, he would have killed me already.

I'm looking at the boy near the newsstand. He is shaking and waiting for me in the snow. What's the point of all this? The war will never end.

In the end, the Germans will defeat all of us, the Russians, the Americans, the resistance, me, I know that. The maps of the beaches I see at night, while waiting to be caught, tell me this. The never-ending lines of German soldiers in the boulangerie tell me this, even the food and wine Herr Ernest brings me every time he comes tell me that.

"Cigarette pack, please." I stand at the stall, moving from foot to foot

to keep warm while the seller looks
sideways nervously.

"The price has gone up. Are you
paying in Francs or Reichsmark?"

"Whichever suits you," I pull my
wallet out of the bag and pay
him in silence, then start walking
towards the bridge, lighting a
cigarette to warm up a bit.

The soles of my shoes are already
worn, and the cold from the
pavement freezes my feet, but
I hide it from Oberst Ernest, not
wanting him to rush and buy me a
new pair or to put German money
on the dresser again.

By the bridge, I pass a hunched
family, wrapped in old coats and
torn blankets. Where is my family?
How come I haven't heard yet
from Mom and Dad and Jacob?

At least they do not know where I ended up and what I had to do to survive. Mom would yell at me, and Dad would shut up, but the look in his eyes would tell me how disappointed he was in me.

"What's the point?" I crush the cigarette with the tip of my shoes, and after a few minutes I light another one, my fingers shaking from the cold. The only white dress I'll be wearing will be the snow that will cover my grave, like Claudine's. I should start getting used to it from now on, and I stand in the cold before entering the alley, letting the snowflakes fall on my hair.

We have not met for so long. What does it matter what he says?

"They are building new barriers here and here." My fingers show him the places on the crumpled map he pulled out of his coat pocket, carefully flattening it with his fingers. "If your American friends do not hurry, they will have no place to invade."

"We have to be patient. We have no other choice. I promise you they will come, is everything fine? I'm worried about you." Philip puts down the pencil with which he marked what I said, never letting me write. If someone gets their hands on the map, it could be a death sentence for me.

"No, you are not," I snatch the pencil and begin to fill in the map of the beach with the barrier lines. Perhaps my time has come.

"What are you doing?" Philip tries to stop me, holding my hand.

"No, you are not," I shout and scratch his hand, continuing to write, even though I no longer know what.

"What am I not?" His hands grip me tightly, and I can hear the creaking of the wooden table and chairs on the floor of the damp basement space.

"You are not worried about me at all. It's the telegrams you care about, that's all I'm worth for you. He's making me a Christmas tree and talking to me about Germany and family, and you are interested in telegrams. You didn't even ask our Communist friends what happened to my family."

"They are in Auschwitz. Your Ernest and his friends sent them to Auschwitz," he shouts back at me, looking at me with anger and hatred.

"I know they arrived at the Auschwitz camp."

"No one comes back from Auschwitz, and more and more trains with people are going there. Do you understand what that means?" I can hear his shouts echo in me from the walls closing around, unable to believe what he is telling me.

"So why didn't you tell me when you knew?" My breathing is heavy. I have to sit down, inhale. This basement is suffocating me. "Why didn't you tell me?"

"How could I tell you such a thing?" He tries to hug me while his voice breaks. "How could I tell you?"

I can't be here anymore. Where's the door outside? I have to breathe, where are the stairs?

"Who will want me?" I've been left alone, let me get out of here, don't touch me. My hands push him. Please, stop staring at my tears running down my cheeks over Mom and Dad and Jacob and the name that makes me sick of Auschwitz, and Herr Oberst Ernest, and me, for all I did when they were no more. I feel sick.

"I want you."

"No one will want me, don't you understand?" I try to fight him off. I have no more Mom and Dad.

"I will want you, it will end one day, and I will study at the Sorbonne as I once did, and we will all return as we once were." He insists on hugging me.

"The past is dead, gone, even you once said it," I shout at him and cry, "no one can fix it."

"But I still want you." He refuses to release me.

"I do not want to see you anymore. Find yourself a replacement, someone whose fingers have no stains of paint and the smell of gun oil." I get up from the hard floor and search for the stairs.

"Please, don't go."

"Don't you understand? I do not want to see you anymore, ever. Get out of my life. I'm like the rats in the Nazi movies, everyone I touch dies or leaves. I spread diseases. I slept with a German officer; you will never marry me. I am an infected Jew."

To Live

March, 1944

Secret 3/5/1944

From: Western Front Wehrmacht Command

To: Army Group France

Subject: Preparations for an attack in the West

Background: Army units subordinate to the Western Front must be on alert for an American-British invasion attempt on French shores.

General: France's citizens are expected to show signs of ingratitude towards the German army and may attempt to provoke rebellion in anticipation of the coming liberation. Army units must impose severe discipline on the population and search for ungrateful civilians.

Tasks:

1. Army officers should be alert to treason attempts by locals.

2. It is the army officers' responsibility to instill the German army's power in the local population.

SS. Telegram 93

The Sewing box

"My dear, I lost a button on my uniform. Will you sew it back on for me?"

"Certainly, my dear." Herr Ernest hands me his grey-green shirt, the one with the black iron cross, and remains in a white tank top. Carefully I take the metal button from his hand and walk to the bedroom, searching for a sewing kit. We have not met since that time in the basement three months ago.

It's better for me that way, trying not to think about him anymore. I even stopped wandering the streets aimlessly, smoking, looking to punish myself, strolling without direction until the curfew hour. The sketchbook pages are full of new intelligence, hidden in code names among all the flower drawings. But all the information I received didn't change anything, and even if I wanted to contact him, I don't know how. It's better for me, without looking at his fingers or remembering the smell of his shirt.

"Darling? Did you find a sewing kit?" Herr Ernest's voice coming from the study takes me back to reality, and I sit down by the bed, opening the dresser drawers one by one, searching for a sewing kit. I remember seeing one when we moved here, along with the few things that were left in the apartment.

The wooden box is hidden in the third drawer, between white tablecloths. It is made of mahogany wood, and I place it on my lap, looking in the small drawers for a green-grey thread, comparing the small spools to the shirt spread out on the bed. Another drawer opens, and another, as I rummage through with my fingers, pulling from the bottom, and suddenly I notice them and freeze.

Like a snake bite, I quickly close the box. The sound seems to shake the whole room.

"Is there a thread in the right color?"

"I found something similar." My voice is shaking. Did he notice?

Slowly, carefully, I open the small wooden drawers again, gently pulling the spools and trying to peek, quietly praying that I am wrong, but they are there, in the bottom drawer, under some burgundy spools of thread.

I send my fingers out, touch them, pull the spools aside, expose them to the warm air in the room, gently feeling the yellow cloth with my fingertips, and drawing the outline of the letters 'Juif' in the center of the Star of David.

"My dear, I'm in a hurry. I have an appointment."

"I just found it. I'm sewing it right now. I almost forgot how to sew."

"A good woman never forgets," his voice came from the study.

My trembling hands fail again and again to insert the grey thread into the eye of the needle. It is pushed aside with each tremor, refusing to lock itself, and the tears are interrupting it as well.

"I'll be done in a minute."

My fingers sew quickly, pushing the needle firmly into the stiff, rough cloth, ignoring the pain of stabbing it into the shirt, loop after loop, non-stop, like an emotionless machine. Still, in the middle of sewing, I can't anymore. I toss the shirt aside, gripping the wooden box and pouring all its contents onto the bed with a great noise, not thinking what will happen if Herr Ernest loses his patience and comes to find the source of the noise. My fingers rummage through the box, checking to see if there is anything left in the empty wooden cells, but there is almost nothing else there. Just the two yellow badges and one light brown photo of a family by the sea. A father and mother and two children sitting on the small stones, and on the other side, it is written in pencil: "Us, June 5th, 1939, the hotel in Nice."

"Were you crying?" he asks as I stand at the study entrance, handing him the ironed uniform with the button back in place.

"No, I just rubbed my eyes. I couldn't get the thread into the needle."

"Well, thank you very much. Too bad it took you so long. I have to leave now. The driver is already waiting outside."

"Will we meet in the evening?"

"Yes, Please wait for me." He

reviews himself in the hall mirror, making sure the button is back in place. His presence in the small entrance hall is too dense for me, but before I can breathe, I have to wait until I hear the door slam shut behind him and the sound of his footsteps moving down the stairwell. I must go out and feel some air that is not in this apartment, a place that does not have a German officer's presence and the smell of eau de cologne.

But I can't return the yellow badges in my pocket to their hiding place in the sewing box, nor the light brown photo.

***

"May a loving man give you a flower," my lips whisper as I pretend to place a flower on her grave, my hand empty. I couldn't find any flowers. The older woman wasn't standing on the corner, and I do not know what happened to her. Maybe she did not survive the winter, or perhaps she went looking for loving couples in another place. Who would buy flowers when there was no money for food, and the German soldiers were at the front?

The square overlooking the Eiffel is also deserted. The smiling German soldiers and the French girls like me, hanging on their arms, have gone. Only a few army trucks pass through the square in a slow drive, rushing to their destination on the western front, not stopping to buy flowers for anyone.

The cemetery is quiet, and I clean the stone with my hand, brushing it as hard as I can even though the winter rain has washed it clean.

"Sorry I haven't been here for a long time. I'll tell you everything," my lips start mumbling as I try to stop my tears, but I cannot tell her. I can't say the words out loud. Even the yellow badge hiding in my dress pocket does not give me enough courage.

"Exalted and hallowed be His great Name," my lips mumble the prayer to the souls of Mom and Dad and Jacob, and I do not know more than these words. I do not know if I am allowed to pray because I am a woman, and it is not acceptable, and I'm committing a great sin, as Dad used to tell me when I refused to light candles on Friday night, yelling at him that I was French and did not want to be Jewish, but I do not care.

My lips repeat the few words I do know in a whisper, over and over, as I hold the yellow badge firmly in my fists, my eyes closed.

"Sorry, Claudine, I have not visited you in so long. I will come more," I apologize before I walk away from the grave. For a moment, my gaze is turned back as I struggle with the urge to leave the yellow badge on the stone, but it's too dangerous. I must return it to its hiding place.

I have to see someone I'm running away from; maybe she will agree to take me back.

***

What if she refuses to open the door for me? I stop at the avenue and look around. Maybe I should stay here? Between the cafés I'm already familiar with?

The German laughter from last spring has disappeared, and only a few soldiers are sitting at the empty tables, served by bored waiters. Maybe I'll sit for a few minutes? Perhaps it's not a good idea to go to her?

What could I tell her? After I ran away from her without saying goodbye? Packing my few belongings and disappearing from her life without explaining, I have not even called her since, even though her luxurious apartment has a telephone. I tried to pick up the phone and ask for her several times, but once I heard the operator's voice asking me for the number, I slammed the black tube back into place.

I have to hurry, Oberst Ernest will come soon, and he doesn't like to wait for me. Recently, his green eyes have become cold, and his voice sounds sharp, making me even more nervous. I quickly cross the boulevard, looking away from the Arc de Triumph and the Nazi flag flying overhead.

The narrow streets have not changed as I walk through them; even the large metal door at the entrance remains as it was. What will she say to me? Maybe I'll go back and return another day?

My fists clenched, and my nails pressing hard into the palms of my hands, I wait by the door after ringing the bell. My stomach hurts.

She's not there. I can go now, at least I tried. But the door opens, and she is standing and looking at me.

"My girl, you have grown so much." I hear her voice as her hands wrap around me warmly, and I let the tears come out.

"I'm a Jew," I sob in the stairwell.

"Shhh... shhh... it's okay... be careful that no one hears." She pulls me inside, and closes the door behind us.

"I am a Jew, and they sent my parents to a place called Auschwitz in the east, and probably killed them." I can't stop whimpering and crying.

"It's okay, my girl, it's okay," she continues embracing me. "They're watching over you from above, hugging you from there."

"I miss them so much, and I'm with a German officer. I live with him. I'm so ashamed. He brings me food." My face is red and wet from the tears, and my body is shaking and whimpering, vomiting out all the shame I've carried inside for so long.

"Shhh... shhh... it's okay." Her hands continue to stroke my hair, trying to calm me down.

"I just wanted to stay alive and look where I ended up..." My voice choked.

"Shhh... my beautiful girl... no one wants to die..." She continues to hug me as I calm down, and only my breaths are heard inside the luxurious guest room.

"Shall I make us a cup of tea? Or coffee? I think I even have some real coffee left."

"What will I do?" I ask her sometime later, as we sit in her living room, sipping the tea she made for us. Now and then, I still have to wipe away a tear, but I am not shaking anymore.

"Move on, just keep moving on. You have to stay alive."

"I cannot live like this. I can't go back to him."

"Can you leave him?"

"They will catch me and kill me."

"So you must go back, for yourself, for your parents who are watching you from above, for Claudine, for Philip, for all the people who care about you. You are not alone. Even if sometimes you feel you have no one, you must live for them."

"How will I do that?"

"Just keep moving on the best you can, the liberation will arrive, the Americans will come."

"I no longer believe they will ever invade. The Germans always win in the end."

"The war will be over, you must believe, if not for you, for them."

"And what about you? Do you believe the war will end?"

"Sometimes it's hard for me too,

but then I imagine what he would do or say," she smiles at me sadly and looks at the man in the picture above the fireplace, "so yeah, I probably keep living for him."

We say goodbye with a warm hug, and I hurry home, knowing I'm late and that Oberst Ernest will be angry with me. Why did she mention Philip? How does she know about him? But I do not have time to think about it; he sent me to her house, and Lizette surely heard about him. I have to hurry, Herr Ernest is waiting for me.

"I need to move on. The war will end soon," my lips repeatedly whisper as I speed up my steps. The apartment is already close.

"Where were you?" He looks up from the documents placed in front of him, lying on the massive oak desk in his study, the room I am not allowed to enter.

"I was delayed. I apologize."

"I'm waiting for you, we'd made plans to go to a show, and I came especially."

"I know, I'm sorry."

"I have a lot of work to do. War is not a distant concept. It is approaching us. You have to understand that."

I silently dress, not wanting him to be angrier at me than he is already. The drive to the theater passes silently with his gloved hand resting on my thigh.

"It is always such a pleasure
to again meet the French
mademoiselle who speaks perfect
German," the senior officer smiles
at me in his black uniform with
a skull on his visored hat, as we
stand at the theater hall entrance.

"Germany above all," I answer him
in perfect German.

"I am always happy to meet a loyal
French citizen."

"I hope not in the building on
Avenue Foch," another officer joins,
and everyone around laughs, but
Herr Ernest says nothing.

"Where are you going?" Oberst
Ernest asks me when I turn my
back and start walking.

"To the ladies' room."

Don't be afraid of him. He is just flirting with you. He knows nothing. I wash my face with cold water, but it doesn't help. I have to go back. They are waiting for me.

"Sorry, I had a nauseous moment." I return to the group of officers again, hoping Herr Ernest won't smell the cigarette I smoked in the restroom.

"We hope you are not cooking us a little German kid," an armored officer winks at me, and I get close to Herr Ernest, holding his arm.

"Well, about that, you'd have to ask my Herr Ernest." I smile a perfect red lipstick smile at the officer. Even though everybody is laughing, Herr Ernest is looking at me with his green eyes and not smiling.

I'm not pregnant. Anaïs already taught me how to be careful, when I still had to learn what to do. "Take this, it's for you, so you won't have to donate a child to the Führer." She placed a pack of rubbers in my hands, explaining to me how to use them as I blushed and hurried to hide them in my bag. "I'm just making sure you don't come to me later, asking for my help." She laughed and lit a cigarette for herself, then, before I started to smoke.

"Here's to German women who devote their wombs to the Fatherland." I fake a smile.

"Here's to German women." The officers around me agree, smelling of cologne, and even Herr Ernest raises his glass.

"Let's go inside." Herr Ernest holds my arm as the announcer rings the bell, and we all head to our seats.

"I look forward to our next meeting," the black-uniformed officer kisses my hand politely as I tightly hold Oberst Ernest's arm, waiting for the lights to go out.

Soon the war will be over. Lizette promised me that. But I have not seen Philip since I shouted at him in the basement.

***

A few days later, I'm walking by the newsstand when I notice the boy is back. He is arranging a pile of newspapers and whispering to me about the meeting point, and my heart is pounding. It's been so long.

I must not think about Philip; I have to concentrate, make sure I am not followed in the streets. What about my fears of Herr Ernest? Shall I tell him? Will he calm me down after all the horrible things I said to him?

The road to the Latin Quarter does not end as I pedal the bike, hurrying as fast as I can, looking down in shame as I pass a long line of women. They are waiting quietly at the grocery store entrance, hoping to buy some food with their food ration stamps.

I will tell him everything, even if nothing will ever be between us, and even if all he is interested in is the information I'm bringing. I don't care; he is waiting for me.

The stairs leading down into the basement seem dark, and I stand and arrange my breath, my dress, the bag strap on my shoulder, and I brush my hair with my fingers; I am ready, despite the dull ache in the bottom of my stomach. Will he hug me?

Without thinking, I quickly go down the stairs, stopping on the last step, looking at him and freezing. He is not Philip.

"Hello, Monique," the stranger standing at the basement entrance reaches his hand out. "Do not run away."

***

The Stranger

Where's Philip? What did they do to him? Did they catch him? Is this man German? I want to scream, and my stomach hurts. What should I do?

Think fast about a cover story. My hand quickly goes into my dress pocket, but all I have is a yellow badge. Why didn't I put it back in its place? They will kill me. Where's Philip?

"Everything is fine," the stranger raises his hand in a calming motion and tells me his name, but with all the screams in my head, I can hear nothing.

"Monique," he tries to approach.

Slowly, I go back up the stairs.

"Do not run away. Everything is fine. I'm one of ours. I'm replacing Philip."

Everything is not fine, and I do not believe him, where's Philip? My hand stays tucked in my dress pocket, holding the yellow badge tightly; maybe he'll think I have a weapon, while my eyes follow his movements, ready to run away, even though he will probably shoot me if I turn my back.

"Everything's fine, do not be afraid, I'm replacing Philip, and I'll work with you from now on." He smiles at me, but I can hear noises outside in the street upstairs.

"Where's Philip?" I slowly approach the wooden table waiting for us in the basement, watching him come closer and raise his hand again.

Then, in one movement, I kick him as hard as I can, turning around and escaping up the stairs. Between my breaths, I can barely hear him groaning behind me, and the sound of a falling chair, but I'm not stopping; I must run out of here.

Like a bullet, I burst into the street and start to run as fast as I can, almost tripping over the smooth street stones, trying to pass through two merchants arguing, holding wooden carts, and shouting at each other for the right to cross the narrow street. I don't have time to look back.

In one of the alleys, I hide and rest for a few minutes, leaning against the cracked brick wall and trying to catch my breath. What was that? What happened to Philip?

Did they ambush me? I carefully peeked into the main street, but everyone seemed suspicious. The man dozing on the bench and the woman standing in the store's doorway, and what about the young man slowly pedaling his bike, looking to the sides, is he looking for me?

My head is down as I return to the main street, trying to walk calmly. Running earlier was a mistake; it surely attracted attention. I don't want them to find me. I promised Lizette that I would stay alive.

"What arrived today?" I ask the last woman in line as I stand behind her, waiting on the street to enter the grocery store, hoping I'm not arousing suspicion with my modern dress.

"They say he had bread and oil, but there is not much left."

"I hope something will be left by the time we get inside," I smile at her while looking to the sides of the street.

"He does not accept the old coupons, only the new ones. Do you have the new ones?"

"Yes, I have."

"Would you like to exchange coupons?" she whispers to me, not wanting the others standing in the line to hear us. "I can give you cheese coupons in exchange for meat coupons, is it right with you?"

"Yes, sure." My fingers rummage in my bag, searching for the ration card as I turn my back on her and carefully tear off the stamps. I don't want her to notice that my ration card is almost unused, it will arouse her suspicions, and she will start poking around, asking more questions. The street is empty, maybe I've managed to escape from them.

"What a fool I am. I've run out of oil coupons. I'm standing here for nothing." I make a sad face.

"Never mind, I'll give you one of mine," she smiles at me. "We women must help each other. Otherwise, how will we survive this war?"

The sun has already set as I cross Pont Neuf towards the east bank, holding a paper bag with a loaf of bread. The metro has already stopped operating at such an hour, they are trying to save electricity, and I will have to walk all the way to the apartment. At least I insisted on giving her some meat stamps from my ration card, knowing they are priceless, and I do not need them anyway. My pantry is full of German army meat tins.

On the way home, I occasionally stop and look back, making sure I am not being followed. Sometimes I sit on a bench in the avenue, resting and looking around, but I avoid smoking, even though I need it so much. A smoking woman always draws attention.

Carefully I approach the building and carefully climb the stairs and listen outside the door. The apartment is dark and empty. No one is waiting to arrest me, not even Herr Oberst Ernest. He informed me he would not come today. He's been coming less recently.

I wake up at night, hearing someone outside on the building stairs, but no one knocks loudly at the door, shouting at me to open up. What happened to Philip? Maybe I'm wrong, and everything's okay? Perhaps he's replacing him? I did not even manage to hear the stranger's name.

Next time I will be more prepared.

***

The next day, on my way out from the boulangerie, the boy is waiting for me again, and I have to go back to the Latin Quarter. I'm ready this time.

Step by step, I carefully go down the stairs, my hand resting in my dress pocket, my fingers firmly holding the knife's handle. The yellow badge was returned to its hiding place in the sewing kit. I must never repeat such mistakes.

Along the way, I was still hoping it was a mistake or a bad dream and that Philip would be waiting for me this time, but it wasn't a dream. The same stranger is waiting for me in the damp basement.

"Hello, Monique."

I remain standing on the last step, nervously examining him, and say nothing. I must know what happened to Philip.

"Hello again." He tries to get closer but notices the tiny movement of my body stepping back, and stops where he is, afraid I'll run away or try to kick him again. My fingers hold the knife's handle tighter.

"I am listening."

"I'm replacing Philip."

"And why does he need a replacement, and where is he?"

"I can't tell you."

"So why should I believe you?"

"You have to believe me. Look, he gave this to me." And the stranger takes the map of the Normandy coastline out of his pocket, places it on the table, the same map I tried to draw the last time we met. I'm so sorry for what I said to him.

"Did you replace him because of what I said to him?"

"What did you say to him?"

"Doesn't matter."

"Are you ready to get closer?"

"Will he meet me again?"

"I do not know. It doesn't depend on me."

"What is your name?" I ask him in German.

"I do not understand," he answers me in French. Shall I believe him?

On the way back to the city's east bank, I choose to return through Pont des Arts. The river's grey water flows quietly under the wooden boards, and despite the chill wind, I sit on one of the benches and light myself a cigarette. A couple of adults standing not far from me are looking at me and whispering, but I ignore them, feeling the hot smoke in my throat. I have already done much worse than smoking. Am I falling into the trap of the Gestapo? Did they infiltrate the resistance? Doesn't he want to see me anymore?

"Do not cry, my dear. He will return." The older woman who looked at me with anger earlier is approaching me. "Everything will be all right."

"Thanks." I smile at her, wiping my tears with the handkerchief she's handed me. He will come back, he must come back, I will bring the best information I can get, and I will stay alive, telling him how much I miss him.

Before they walk away, the older woman turns to me, smiling one last time for encouragement, and I smile back at her, wiping my tears again. I have to stop this crying; Herr Ernest will arrive at the apartment soon. He wants us to go out with his officers, and I need to continue acting like everything is perfect.

*****

The dark night sky is filled with the lights of anti-aircraft trace ammunition slowly climbing up, until they disappear between the clouds.

"Stop the vehicle," Oberst Ernest instructs the driver as we hurry to get out of the car, rushing to the side of the street and looking up.

I can't see the American bombers in the dark night, nor the German searchlights traveling between the clouds and looking for them, but I can feel them there, in the sky above me.

Their monotonous noise and the echoes of explosions in the distance make me sweat and cower in fear while I cover my head with my hands.

The street is entirely dark, the few lamps that are still on at night have gone out, as ordered, and I kneel on the dark, cold sidewalk.

"Come on, hurry up," he calls to me, and I continue in the direction of his voice, clinging to the wall, waiting to feel the heat of the bombs, but they do not come.

The sirens' howls don't stop, tearing at my ears, but the anti-aircraft batteries aren't heard at all at a distance. Only their death bullets are seen, painting the skies in red stripes. The bombers are probably just passing by.

"You can get up. It's over." Herr Ernest reaches his hand out after a few minutes, supporting me as I get up from the sidewalk, arranging my evening dress. "Your friends went to bomb other Frenchmen."

"I'm with you, and they're bombing me too. I do not support the Americans."

"I know you are loyal to the German nation." He opens the car door for me; did he mean what he said?

The rest of the ride passes quietly, with the car's headlights making their way through the dark streets to the nightclub, but his hand does not rest on my thigh.

"I thought you would not come," Anaïs hugs me and shouts in my ear, trying to overcome the noisy music.

"Slight delay," I smile and point up with my finger.

"Yes, soon they will arrive, and then we all have to learn English." She smiles her knowing smile.

"I'm not going to replace what I have." I place my hand on Herr Ernest's back, as he is busy talking to the Fritzes. Even though we have not exchanged a word since the unplanned stop on the street, I must have him trust me.

"We will see." She laughs at me and hugs her Fritz, whispering something in his ear, and he takes a cigarette box out of his pocket, lighting one for her.

"How are you?" I try to shout to Violette, who is sitting quietly on the other side of the table, but she does not answer me; she just smiles sadly.

"Lately, Fritz doesn't give her attention at all," Anaïs volunteers to tell me the latest news, ignoring Violette who is sitting beside her.

"She's afraid he won't take her with him to Germany." And I feel sorry and want to hug her. She looks so lost to me.

"Do not worry, Violette, he will stay here with us until the end." Anaïs hugs her instead of me. "Look what the city has to offer him," she points to the stripper dancing in front of the men. She is wearing panties and shaking her breasts, which are bound in a purple corset, to the cheers of the crowd. "No one else will be able to provide him with such pleasure."

Anaïs' evil surprises me, and I look for something to answer her, but Violette gets up and walks towards the restroom, pushing between the crowds, women in nightdresses and men mostly in German uniforms.

"She does not need you, she needs to face reality," Anaïs grabs my arm as I get up, intending to follow her. "She needs to learn how to take care of herself, like us."

"I'll be right back." I smile at her, hurrying after Violette into the dim opening on the side of the stage, apologizing to the people around the tables as I pass. I'm running out of friends to lose.

"He's ignoring me," she cries in front of the filthy mirror, and her whole body trembles as she searches through her little bag, looking for a pencil to fix the makeup around her eyes. "He tells me I don't support him enough and that he's busy."

"Maybe he's busy?"

"A few days ago, he returned to town, and we haven't met since then." Her sobs continue.

"Men are like that," my hand touches her shoulder. "They like to play in the war." The feeling of the mature woman who should encourage another is strange to me.

"He was not like that at first. At first, he had time to hang out with me, promising me things."

"That's the way it is. First they promise you things until they get into your underwear, but after that, they are not interested." I try to speak with a funny tone, but Violette just cries more.

"What will they do to me?" She turns to me with a scared look, her cheeks dirty from her smeared eye makeup.

"Who?" My hand continues to caress her shoulder, even though it feels strange to me.

"Everyone, the French."

"I don't understand."

"What will they do to me if the Russians or the Americans come?" I stop caressing her.

"They will not come, they have been fighting for four years, and they have not come yet."

"I was so scared today when I heard the bombers coming. I didn't want to come at all, but Fritz insisted."

"The Germans are strong. They will beat the Americans if they come.

Nothing will happen to you. Your Fritz will protect you."

"And the Russians?"

"They will defeat the Russians too."

"It all happened because of the Jews who control the world's economy. They influenced the Russians with their money, and now the Americans too." She wipes her face with a handkerchief she pulled out of her bag, looking at herself in the mirror. She has never really been my friend.

"I heard that the Germans have done unspeakable things as well." I can't stop myself.

"Those are just rumors. I do not believe that my Fritz would harm someone; he is so polite with me even when he is angry, not like

French men." She fixes her lipstick and, unhappy with the result, removes it with her handkerchief, applying it again.

"They are probably just rumors. They will not come. You will stay with your Fritz forever, you will see." I force myself to hug her a little for encouragement, waiting for her to finish fixing her makeup, but she already wants to return to the club. Suddenly the noisy club feels intimate to me, despite the loud music, the applause, and the cigarette smoke filling it.

"Did you hold her hand while she was fixing her makeup?" Anaïs whispers as we sit down at the table. "Don't worry," she brings her mouth close to mine, making sure I hear her over the noise, "I hosted a company for everyone instead of you. What are best friends for?"

But it does not seem to me that the men are paying any attention to her at all. Though she never stops stroking her Fritz's back, the men's eyes are focused on the almost-naked dancer on the stage. She slowly removes her skirt to the sounds of cheers and whistles. No one from the crowd cares anymore about the dark planes that passed over our heads earlier tonight.

Later, in the apartment bedroom, I wonder if, like all men, Herr Ernest lays on me but imagines the stripper shaking her breasts in front of his eyes and mostly smiling at him, impressed by his high rank. When he was in Russia, did he own some woman? Doing horrible things during the day and being polite to her at night? The same politeness he shows me?

The sound of Herr Ernest's
breathing disturbs the silence
in the room as I sneak into the
forbidden study. I must find better
information, to see Philip again.

***

Fissures

"The Germans are moving more forces towards the coast and splitting headquarters. There is an argument between the generals."

"What kind of argument?"

"Something about unit sectors, I could not understand."

"And how do you know that?"

"I heard a phone call."

"Monique, you've done a good job so far, but these are things that we are less interested in. I need you to get me plans, photos, not rumors you maybe hear in a casual phone conversation."

"I'm bringing anything I can get my hands on."

"Monique, you need to work harder. We need every bit of information for the coming invasion, not just pieces of small talk. I need you to get me maps, telegrams, real material." His finger knocks on the wooden table that separates us, making me cringe. It seems to me that he hasn't forgiven me for the kick he received at our first meeting. I can apologize to him, but he's still scaring me.

"When will Philip return?"

"I'm replacing him. You're working with me now."

"Yes, but when will he return?"

"What does it matter to you? Are you working for Philip, or the resistance and the liberation of France?"

His black eyes angrily stare at me as I curl up in my chair, lowering my gaze slightly and examining his clean grey button-down shirt.

"I am working for the resistance."

"You should forget about Philip; for you, he no longer exists."

My fingers tighten around the knife handle in my dress pocket, unable to release the grip and place my hands on the table. But he is also sitting in front of me with his hands tucked deep in his pants pockets, taking them out only when he wags his fingers and scolds me. Why does Philip not want to meet me anymore? I have to find him.

"Monique, you are not listening to me."

"Sorry, what did you say?"

"That you must be more efficient, certainly if you want to go back and work with Philip." His finger is raised again in front of my face.

"I'll be more efficient, I promise." But I keep my hand in my dress pocket.

On my way out, I look for the little girl from the shop in the alley. I have two cans of canned milk that Herr Ernest brought me. She will probably relish the white sweetness; surely she needs the milk more than I do. The girl in the torn shoes and dirty dress approaches me in hesitating steps and stares suspiciously at my hands holding the two white cans, on which German eagles are printed, holding black swastikas.

"Take it," I whisper to her, and she snatches them from my hand and runs from me, laughing as if she doesn't care about the war and the Germans spreading fear.

I don't remember myself laughing. I think I forgot how to laugh when I saw my first German soldier a few days after the occupation. He stood on our street corner and ordered Dad to bow to his hobnail boots before we could continue walking. We were on our way home, and I held Dad's hand and smiled awkwardly at the soldier.

"What are you laughing at?" The huge soldier shouted at me in German, waving his arm and threatening me as I looked up at him and choked.

"It's okay," Dad whispered to me, humiliated and bowing before the soldier let us continue our way, not before throwing Dad's hat on the pavement, forcing him to kiss the ground.

"Let's go home. Mom made you something delicious." He tried to cheer me up, but from that day on I did not laugh anymore.

"Don't cry," Dad tried to soothe me. "Mom's waiting for us at home." Our home with the red carpet in the living room and the kitchen that was always full of cooking aromas. The house that must have been taken over by a German officer housing his mistress.

Is one of the rooms set as his study, which she is not allowed to enter, but she does by night?

***

My fingers quickly go over the pile of documents in his briefcase as I carefully pull them out and carry them with me to the bathroom. Quietly I sit on the floor and read them by candlelight, trying to understand the assessments for protection from a telegram allocating barbed wire fences to various shorelines.

The noise of the bathroom handle makes me jump out on the floor, and I manage to blow out the candle.

"What are you doing?" I hear his voice through the closed door.

"I'm in here." What to do? I'm dead, my hands hold the candle, what to do with it? And all the telegrams?

"What are you doing in there?"

"I need to be here."

"I've been lying awake in bed for a long time, waiting for you." What to answer him? What about the pages? My hands search in the dark, looking for somewhere to tuck them in. What if they wrinkle? He will kill me.

"Please don't come in. I'm so ashamed. I ate something bad." My fingers grope and carefully push the papers behind the radiator before I go out and quietly close the door behind me.

"Please do not go in, I beg you." My eyes try to examine his silhouette in the darkness of the room, but after a moment, I choose to turn my back on him and quietly walk to bed; he mustn't think I am trying to stop him from entering the bathroom.

With every step, I wait to hear him open the door or grab me by the hair and throw me on the floor for turning my back on him, but when I lie in bed and finally stop shaking, he joins me.

Only hours later, when I'm sure he is well asleep, I get up again and carefully return the telegrams to his leather bag, praying he will not notice that they are more wrinkled than they were before. I won't do that anymore. It's getting too dangerous.

"Are you okay? Aren't you sick?" Simone asks me the next morning.

"No, I'm okay, everything is fine."

"Then why are you late again? The fact that you are living with a

German officer doesn't give you special privileges. Ordinary citizens have more to struggle with than you. Look at Marie. She is always on time."

I apologize to Mrs. Simone and hurry to stand behind the counter, waiting for the day to end so I can go back to the apartment, put my head down, and get some sleep.

***

The sound of the vase shattering on the floor wakes me in a panic, and I sit up in bed, trying to figure out what's going on. My eyes are wide open, but I see nothing in the dark room. In the distance, there is a muffled noise of an explosion followed by a flash of light from the window, penetrating the room's curtain, followed by a much louder explosion that shakes the iron bed and the window. I bend over and scream, covering my head with my hands. What's going on?

Another flash from the window, followed by a deafening explosion; I can hear the sobs of sirens from a distance, and the cups in the kitchen shattering on the floor. As I stumble from the bed to the floor, I cover my head with my hands, clinging to the wooden floor, making myself as small as I can, trying to disappear inside the parquet. I do not want to die.

Another explosion shakes the house while I crawl towards the window, getting on my knees and opening it. What's going on outside? The explosions blast wave immediately blows the window from my hand, slamming it against the wall, pulling back the curtain, and all the sounds of hell enter the room. The next house's windows sparkle with orange light, fire reflected from a distance, and the skies are lit in red-orange colors. Anti-aircraft batteries are firing lines of red tracer ammunition in a monotonous rumble, painting red dots towards the orange sky, but above all, there is the noise of growls and explosions.

Like a deep gurgle that does not stop for a moment, the noise of the aircraft bomber engines in the sky fill the air as they pass in an endless stream of invisible monsters above me in the darkness, growling incessantly with a muffled voice of rage.

Another explosion shakes the air, and I am thrown back, screaming. Please don't hit the house. While crawling on the floor and ignoring the porcelain shards of the vase wounding me, I manage to find my nightgown and make my way in the dark to the front door. Another flash, followed by an explosion, illuminates my way for a moment. I must escape.

My hands fight to unlock the door, sliding them by force, but the key falls to the floor with a sharp sound of metal, and I grope for it with my wounded hands, crying for them not to kill me. Please move on; throw your bombs elsewhere, just not on me. Another explosion shakes the house as I try to insert the key, looking for the keyhole with trembling hands.

Through the open door, I crawl
down the stairs, groping in the
dark and leaning against the
railing. From the stairwell window,
I can see the orange light of
distant fires and more explosions,
painting the air with shards of light
that fly to the skies, making me
cringe in my place on the stairs.
I must reach the bottom, where I
will be safe.

She is kneeling near the third-floor
door, and I almost stumble and fall
when I hit her, screaming in fear,
but bending over and touching
her body. She is silent even as I'm
trying to shake her, feeling her
body trembling under my touch.

"Are you okay?" Another flash of
light from the window highlights
her open eyes that are looking at
me.

"It's the Americans," she answers in a hollow voice.

"Are you okay? Are you injured?"

"They're bombing me."

"Are you okay? Injured? Can you get up?"

"It's the Americans."

"Come, get up, lean on me."

"They're bombing me."

"We must hurry."

"It's the Americans."

"Get up," I scream and slap her, cringing again at the noise of the glass in the stairwell and the never-ending growl of planes. Stop it already. We're both going to die here.

"Get up," I slap her again, and finally, she slowly rises, leaning against my body, and we both go down the stairs, hiding under the staircase at the entrance. While hugging her, I whisper to the planes to go, asking them to leave and cringing with each explosion, knowing the next bomb will hit us.

Long after the growl has gone and disappeared into the night, and only the light of the fires in the city paints the clouds in the night sky grey-orange, we slowly start climbing the stairs again. Occasionally I hear people running in the street, or a fire truck's siren whimpering and disappearing between the buildings in the distance, painted yellow.

"Here, this is your door," I say goodbye to her at the front door of her apartment. "Do you have the key?" Maybe she will hate me less.

"The Americans bombed me." She refuses to let go of her grip, holding me firmly, and I have to take her to my apartment, seating her in the kitchen and making her a cup of tea. I already want to be alone and curl up in bed, even though I cannot fall asleep.

"Are you okay?" I put the cup of tea in front of her.

"Was I scared?"

"No, you were not afraid. You were just fine."

"You have a lot of food." Her gaze wanders to my pantry shelves, filled with cans wrapped in light brown paper and marked with the sign of the German eagle.

"Want some?" And she nods her head. I do not need so much anyway.

"Have a quiet night," I say goodbye to her later at the door of her apartment, helping her down the stairs and supporting her, holding the food I gave her. But after the door slams shut, I am left to sit in the darkness of the stairwell, unable to go up to my apartment alone. I can occasionally hear people outside shouting in the street, or the whistling sound of a passing car.

***

"A barbaric American bomb hits
Paris, the French and the German
nations in a partnership of fate!"
the boy selling newspapers shouts
as he walks down the street and
holds the Paris Soir newspaper
above his head. For a moment,
I want to stop him and tuck a
coin in his hand, and take the
thin newspaper, which contains
government propaganda insults
towards the Americans, but I'm not
sure I can read about people like
me who ran out of luck last night.

The city is quiet this morning;
fewer people walk the streets,
looking to the sides, being careful
not to stumble and get hurt by the
glass scattered on the sidewalks—
even the car traffic, which has
been low lately, is hardly noticeable
this morning. Here and there, I can
hear a fire truck rushing to a fire

that has not yet been extinguished; its horns howl as passersby quietly look at it.

One man stands inside a shattered window in the avenue, quietly collecting the glass remnants into a bucket of tin, gently removing them from the luxury clothes that hang on the dolls in the window, and estimating the damage to his store. Further down the street, several people gather and talk excitedly, recounting the experiences of the previous night, and I stop for a moment.

"I heard the Eighteenth Arrondissement was hit the hardest," one woman babbles to the crowd gathered around her, and I get closer, even though Simone is waiting for me.

"They tried to hit the railroad tracks and hit innocent people," another man adds. "A lot of them got killed." And the crowd nods in approval. I'm already late, and I have to stop listening to them. What if they come again tonight? Or tomorrow?

The sky above is still full of grey smoke, and the burnt smell fills the streets and intensifies as I get closer to the opera and the boulangerie. More people are crowding in groups around the newsstands, reading the headlines and talking excitedly, but I just pass by and do not stop to stand in line. Since yesterday I haven't stopped thinking about Philip. Has something happened to him?

"Thank God you're fine," Simone hugs me as I walk in the door, and

I am embarrassed by the touch of her hands. "I was already afraid something had happened to you. What is going with these Americans and the British? They are unable to come free us, so they decided to try and kill us?" She's trying to be funny, telling a joke I'd heard from someone before on the street, at one of the gatherings.

"They are trying to expel everyone from Paris, so that the city will remain only for them when they come." I also try to contribute to the humor, feeling that I am not succeeding; the boulangerie floor is full of porcelain fragments.

"Come and help me. We'll start cleaning." She hands me the apron and broom, but after consulting with Martin the cook, she calls me to the back room.

"Monique, the butter delivery did not arrive this morning. I do not know what happened to the delivery truck. I want you to go to the market and try to get butter. I will give you our confirmation letter."

For two years now, I have refrained from approaching the massive market building.

For two years, I have circled it or walked the streets around, avoiding the market, fearful that maybe one of the sellers might recognize me from those days I ran from them. Still, Simone refuses to send Marie instead, and I have no choice, I must go there.

I approach the arched structure at the city center, looking down and peeking to the sides. The market is as noisy as ever, though the trucks that used to park on the side streets are gone, and horse-drawn carriages have replaced them. The piles of crates are smaller, or maybe they just stayed huge in my memory as I hid between them, waiting for the night to sneak out for a moment. But the smell of pickled vegetables mixed with cheese and meat has not changed. And the noise and sellers' shouts remain the same.

"My name is Monique Autin," I whisper as I get close to the two policemen standing under the entrance gate of the cheese area, trying to examine their faces. Will they recognize me? But they seem excited, talking about yesterday's bomb with a small man stacking crates of vegetables on a cart, not paying attention at all. They surely are not looking for a single girl who escaped from them two years ago. I take a deep breath and pass them in a steady walk, raising my eyes only when I'm inside and watching all the sellers and the merchandise guards. Step by step, I pace down the first aisle, breathing slowly and pushing between all the people, forcing myself to look around and searching for our butter supplier. My hand tightly holds the confirmation paper that allows him to sell butter to the boulangerie. I mustn't lose it.

"Mademoiselle, he's not here today." The salesman at the next cheese stall returns the crumpled paper to me as he looks at me intently, trying to remember if he knows me.

"Thanks." I snatch the paper from his hand and quickly walk away.

"Maybe he was killed at night, no one knows. Have you bought from him before?"

"Never mind, thanks."

"Mademoiselle, I can sell to you."

"Thanks, I'll manage."

"Mademoiselle, no one else will sell to you, especially after what happened in the night."

What shall I tell Simone? The selection is meager at the cheese stalls, and he is right. They all refuse to look at the paper I'm holding, explaining that their butter is already promised to other stores. Maybe the big man will help me? The one with the filthy tank top and the sour smell of cabbage, who saved my life two years ago and disappeared? What happened to him? Is he with the resistance? I look around, but there's no way I'd recognize him. The market is huge, and I no longer remember where I ran and hid. The rows of stalls and piles of crates look the same to me in every direction my eyes look. And if I find him, will he recognize me and want to help me again?

Finally, I return to the cheese seller with a downcast look, handing him my order and making sure to look around, just not at him, but he keeps examining me as he slices the chunks of butter, as if trying to refresh his memory.

"Thank you," I hurry away from him with the packages on my shoulders.

"You're welcome, come again," he shouts after me, but I no longer answer him.

Only at a safe distance from the market and the two policemen at the entrance do I return to my usual walk. It was just my imagination. There's no way he recognized me from those days I ran hungry between the aisles. I must hurry; Martin is waiting for the butter, but it is difficult to walk down the streets with the stuffy smell of fire all around.

"That's all I've got. It's not enough." I place the baskets in front of Simone.

"I knew I should have sent Marie to do that job. God knows where she disappeared to a few minutes after you left, go and search for her."

"Is everything okay?" I sit next to Marie outside the back entrance of the boulangerie.

"I saw them hitting one of the planes, and the fire coming out of it," she says quietly. "I didn't know where to run."

"They are fighting to set us free."

"I didn't think you would say such a thing." She looks at me.

"Yes, I know what you think of me." I take out a cigarette and light it, smoking in silence, thinking of the American soldiers in the burning bomber who came all the way from overseas to set me free.

"New York, San Francisco, Statue of Liberty," I whisper the magical words of freedom; Dad once showed me postcards from America.

"What did you say?"

"That we need to get back to work. Simone is looking for us." I throw the cigarette and step on it. "Don't worry; they will not return tonight."

***

Paris is not bombed the following nights, but the planes still pass in the dark over the town. I sit in bed and listen to the monotonous noise of their engines, my body tense while I wait to hear the explosions. "Los Angeles, Montana, Niagra Falls," I try to whisper, but my body doesn't stop shaking. Only in the morning do I manage to fall asleep, imagining Philip's warm hands hugging me, like that time in the basement.

There is still a faint smell of fire on the way to work, but they have already cleaned the glass from the streets, and the cracked shop windows are covered with strips of sticky paper. I try to work as hard as I can in the boulangerie, distracting my mind from the nights to come.

The boulangerie door opens, and I notice Violette coming in, her eyes red.

"Good morning," I say, but it's been hard for me to smile since the last time we met at the club about two weeks ago.

"I need to talk to you."

"What happened?" I ask, already guessing that the answer has to do with her Fritz.

"I cannot say." She looks at the soldier waiting in line for his order and watching us.

"Wait. I'll be right with you." I pack his croissants and hope she hasn't gotten Fritz involved in that female problem. Did Anaïs also place a package of rubbers in her hands? Her Fritz probably brings them from German army supply; he wouldn't want to harm his Aryan race's purity, mixing it with some simple local mistress.

"Monique, you are daydreaming. The honorable soldier is waiting."

"Sorry I only gave you only three croissants; we are limited in quantities." I hand the bag to the soldier. Supply shipments have become irregular in recent days, but it does not really matter. The flow of soldiers in grey-green uniforms has filled the small space with loud speeches, and cigarette smoke remains only a distant memory. Only a few of them enter these days. Everyone is at the front, waiting for the invasion, hardly visiting Paris anymore.

"Sit down; I'll join you in a minute." Or maybe Fritz abandoned her, decided she was not right for him. We had not met since that evening at the club, I was comfortable keeping a distance from her, afraid I would be tempted to say nasty things. I've never been like this, maybe I learned from Anaïs, or maybe too much time has passed, and I have become one of them. Surely this is what Simone thinks of me. Even Marie no longer wants to go out for a walk with me on the boulevard, as she wanted to when she was new.

"What happened?" We sit down at one of the empty tables, and even Simone does not make a face. Maybe more customers will enter when they see that people are sitting by the boulangerie tables.

"I can't go on like this anymore."

"What happened?"

"I do not sleep at night, Fritz hardly comes and when he does, he is stressed, there are almost no food rations at the grocery store, and you do not come to visit me."

"I was busy; I apologize." I touch her hand.

"When will they invade?"

"They will not invade."

"I'm scared," she holds my hand. "Why can't we be like we used to be?"

"What do you mean?"

"Back then, when we went to the river, sailed in boats, laughed and had fun, or when we were going to cafés on the Champs-Élysées, and no one cared about when the Americans were coming. I hate this summer."

"The summer has not yet started. We are only at the beginning of June," I answer her, and wonder when exactly, in all this time she was enjoying, Fritz's friends killed my family in Auschwitz. I want to stop stroking her hand, but I hold myself back.

"I already hated this summer before it began," she smiles a little.

"I like to feel your fingers, they're warm, I'm lucky you're my friend."

Two more armored German soldiers enter the boulangerie, laughing and saying they need something sweet before they leave Paris on their way to the staging areas, and Simone clears her throat. I have to get up and serve them.

"Do not worry; the Americans will not come." I give her one last hug before I walk up behind the counter, wondering whether she would have stayed my friend had she known who I really was. "How can I help you?" I ask the two soldiers in the mottled uniforms with a polite smile, the ones who would try to kill the American soldiers if they came to set me free.

On the way back to the apartment, I stop for a few minutes and light a cigarette, walking into one of the small streets, far from the reproachful looks of men seeing a woman smoking, but on the way to the metro, I see several people in long black coats scanning the crowd, and I decide to walk home on foot.

Oberst Ernest informed me that he would come tonight, and I no longer know what scares me more, his presence or the bombers passing through the night sky.

What does it matter, I think to myself when I stop and light another cigarette. My end will be the same.

***

"How was your day?" I kneel at Herr Ernest's feet, trying to help him take off his boots, but he ignores me and enters the apartment, examining it with his eyes.

"What happened to the wine glasses that were in the living room?"

"They were broken a few days ago by the bombers."

"The American and British bombers?" He lets me help him take off his boots.

"Yes, the American and British bombers." I look down at the floor, holding his dirty black boots.

"They are destroying all our achievements, coming at night like thieves, afraid to invade and fight the German army."

"I hate them." I place his hobnail boots by the front door.

"But all the people in the streets cheer when they come."

"I don't think they are cheering for them." I get off the floor and help him remove his coat.

"No, they are spying for information, that's what our intelligence says. They are ungrateful for our efforts to stop the Communist monster coming from the East, destroying the world together with the Jews."

"I hate the Communists."

"The French people always surprise me, supporting the wrong conqueror. Our intelligence reports that the resistance is passing information to England, helping them destroy France."

"I'm with you. I don't want Paris to be destroyed." Is he setting a trap for me? What should I answer?

"Aren't you more French than German?"

"I'm with you here, isn't it the answer?" What should I do? Why did Philip not prepare me for this?

Slowly I hand him back the bottle of wine he brought with him, praying he won't notice my trembling legs, looking into his green eyes and whispering to him in German: "If that doesn't suit you, I can go." Then I turn and walk to the bedroom, getting ready to start packing, my whole body tense and shaking.

Did I do right? Should I have fallen on my knees and begged?

"Take your clothes off."

But I keep walking, turning my back on him, knowing that he is a German officer and he can do whatever he wants to me. He can kill me. No one will even bother to investigate or even ask why he did it. The noise of my footsteps on the parquet floor is jarring to my ears as I keep walking, thinking about my breathing. I don't know what to do, did I made a mistake?

"Please take your clothes off," he gently says to me.

Later, when we are in bed, and he is catching his breath, he apologizes for not reading me poetry for a long time.

"I would love for you to read me poetry. I love German poetry."

"A weak woman would get down on her knees and beg me to forgive her behavior. I hate weak people. Like back then in the East, when I could smell their fear," he whispers, as if to himself, before he gets off me and falls asleep.

The open window and the growl of the planes passing over us leave me awake all night, repeatedly turning restlessly on my side of the bed. Although he is fast asleep, I am too scared to get up and go to his study. Can he smell my fear?

***

The smell of fear is all around me in the next days at the almost-empty boulangerie. I clean the same plates repeatedly or try to get out the back door, sitting in the sun for a while, but Marie never stops talking to me.

"They say the Russian soldiers are the worst. What if they come?" she asks. "The German army radio says we must unite and fight against them."

"Marie, they will not come, they are far away, and according to the German radio, the German army hasn't stopped winning." I lose my patience with her. Even the newspaper headlines keep on publishing German victories, but I don't believe them anymore.

"And they say the Americans will invade Belgium and that the Germans will destroy Paris, just as they destroyed every city before withdrawing."

"Marie, the Russians are in Poland, the Germans are in Paris, they will not destroy Paris. Otherwise they will not have cafés and boulangeries with fresh croissants. Everything will be fine." I get up and enter, waiting for the end of the day. But the boy is waiting for me again at the newsstand. I have to go meet him.

I'm just too tense. I stop for a few minutes over the bridge, trying to calm myself down and checking the people around. It's just the tension that makes me imagine something's wrong. I've been in this costume for too long. It makes sense that I'm scared, especially with all those rumors around, everyone is wondering if there will be an invasion and when.

Everything's okay, I just need to relax.

I carefully go down into the dark entrance to the basement and get ready to meet the man in the grey button-down shirt who is waiting for me. For a moment, I imagine Philip will be standing there with his quiffed hair and old jacket, but I know it will not happen. He will never want me after what I did and said.

"Good afternoon, how are you?" He approaches, wanting to hug and kiss me on the cheek, but I hurry to sit down at the table, feeling more secure with the old wooden board separating us.

"Good afternoon, how are you?"

"I'm good."

"What did you bring with you today?"

"I do not have much information. My officer rarely comes, and we almost don't meet."

"Still, didn't you see or hear anything?"

"They are arguing among themselves whether there will be an invasion or not."

"You told me that last time, we need more information."

He leans back and looks at me angrily. What does he want from me? Doesn't he know that I'm trying? He does not care about all the nights I do not sleep, wondering when they will catch me. About the Gestapo building on 84 Avenue Foch, that I dare not think about at all.

"I will try to do better." My fingers firmly hold the knife in my dress pocket.

"What's your officer's name?"

"Didn't Philip tell you?" He's not my officer, he's German, and I'm scared of him, I'm scared of you too.

"No, Philip told me you would provide me with all the information I would ask for."

"Why are you asking me all these questions?"

"Because the people above me want to know."

"Then ask Philip."

"Don't be rude."

"Sorry."

"And what is his rank?"

"I think he's an Oberstleutnant."

"You do not even know his rank?"

"Their ranks are really confusing. They have so many."

"You are not helping me. What's his last name?"

"I think he's an armored officer. I do not know exactly what unit. I think he's in a Panzer tank."

There is a long moment of silence as we sit on either side of the table, looking at each other. I lower my eyes, trying to think if there is another detail I can tell him that he'd like. Where are his hands? Why does he always keep them in his lap, not putting them on the table as Philip used to do? I have to look up and smile at him, the problem is with me and all the surrounding tension.

 "Is that all you know about him after a year of being together?"

"He does not tell me anything, he is silent."

"You must bring us more material, even if it involves taking more risks."

"I promise I'll try." I choose not to tell him about that time in the bathroom, when Herr Ernest almost caught me.

His dark eyes continue to examine my face and body as if researching me.

"Well, we'll see what to do with you and your poor material." He ends the meeting between us after a few more moments of silence, signaling with his hand that I can go.

"Thanks."

I'll be better. I promise, I want to tell him when I get up, but I say nothing, just turning my back and searching for the stairs. How could I be so wrong about Philip?

The grey light at the end of the stairs seems to invite me to leave this suffocating basement, and I hurry to get out into the open air, feeling his eyes on my back, and letting out a sigh of relief as my feet touch the sidewalk of the alley.

I look for the little girl from the store, wanting to give her a chocolate bar that I brought with me, especially for her. A real chocolate bar, flavored with sweet sugar and bitter cocoa, such that my mouth fills with saliva when I close my eyes and imagine its taste. Even in the German army, they now give chocolate to pilots alone. A few days ago, Herr Ernest brought some chocolate bars with him, placing them in the pantry beside the wine bottles.

But the girl does not peek out the store door, and despite the dripping summer rain, I am ashamed to approach and look inside, preferring to stand and wait for her. I have a bad feeling that something will happen to her and that this is the last time we will meet. Maybe a bomb will hit her, and perhaps something will happen to me.

I need to relax. I will meet her many more times, the sun will soon set, and I have a long walk to the apartment. Herr Ernest has informed me that he will arrive tonight.

***

All night it drizzles, forcing me to close the window. Despite the silence in the dark apartment, I can't fall asleep. My eyes are wide open in the dark room as I listen to his breathing, trying to force myself to walk to his study, but I'm too afraid to get out of bed. The ringing of the phone from the study wakes me up, I must have fallen asleep. While I'm trying to understand what happened in the middle of the night, Herr Ernest is already hurrying to the ringing

phone, listening for a moment
to the sounds coming from the
black tube, putting it in place, and
quickly starting to get dressed.

"What happened?" My hands are
busy tying my bathrobe.

"Nothing special, usual military
alert, go back to sleep." He finishes
zipping his coat, collects the papers
from his desk, perhaps waiting for
me as bait even though I did not
dare approach them. Herr Ernest
stuffs them in his leather bag and
walks out the door, barely saying
goodbye.

The rain has stopped, and I open
the window and peek into the
dark street. A military car passes
and stops for a moment, picking
him up and continuing on its way.
The sound of wheels is heard on

the wet street stones, but after it
disappears behind the street corner
the city returns to its peaceful
night.

On the way to the boulangerie,
the street traffic is usual while
the morning sun dries the wet
sidewalk. Still, inside I hear
Simone's angry voice, talking to
Martin the cook, barely noticing as
I walk through the door, despite
the bell ringing every time it opens.

"This is the fourth time in the
last two weeks that we have not
received butter. How do they
expect us to make croissants? With
their terrible substitutes?"

"Monique," she turns to me,
"please note in the vendor book:
June sixth, and no butter has

arrived again." I go behind the counter, take out the heavy supplier's notebook, writing in perfect handwriting: "June sixth, 1944, no supply of butter."

"Monique, I want you to go to the market again to try and get butter." But I manage to convince her to send Marie, using the excuse that she must gain experience talking to vendors, and soon a lot of soldiers will come, even though the boulangerie is almost empty in recent days.

The morning hours pass lazily by as I help Martin clean the back room when the doorbell rings, and I hear Simone's usual shout in the direction of the baking room: "Monique, you have customers."

My clients are two transport soldiers. I recognize them by the unit badges on their uniforms.

"Good morning, how can I help you?" I ask the two transport soldiers in French, and a minute later, two more soldiers from another unit enter, exchanging greetings, and one of them asks if they heard the radio this morning.

"No," the taller of the two answers, smiling at me flirtatiously.

"The Army radio reported that the enemy has begun an invasion on the beaches of Calais, but we managed to push them back into the sea," the transport soldier tells them and smiles. After a moment of excitement, everyone looks at me and falls silent.

"Have a nice day." I address him in poor German, serving him the bread.

"Thank you." He takes the paper bag from me with a suspicious look.

"How can I help you?" I turn to a soldier who previously tried to smile at me and is now no longer doing so.

"When were the cakes made? This morning?"

"No, unfortunately, they are from yesterday, we have not yet received butter this morning."

"Well, never mind, I'll come later." He and his friend walk out the door.

"What did they say?" Simone asks me the second after the door slams shut.

"They said that the German radio reported an American invasion attempt in the Calais area this morning, and that the attempt failed," I say, and watch the grey morning clouds outside.

"Well, that fits Americans, they can do nothing properly. Where's Marie? Why is she so late?" Simone goes to talk to Martin in the back room, and I think she's wiping a tear away as she passes me.

"All roads from Normandy are blocked," Marie reports excitedly when she finally returns from the market empty-handed. "No delivery truck has come from there since last night, and everyone is whispering that the beach is full of American ships, and there is a war there."

"But the German radio reported on Calais, and you also failed to get butter," Simone silences her.

"That's what they say in the market," Marie apologizes and heads down to the back room in tears.

The rest of the morning passes in silence. A military truck occasionally passes by the boulevard, full of German soldiers. Simone and I accompany them with our gazes and return to cleaning the empty boulangerie tables with cloths.

"Monique, please take care of the cash register. I'll be back soon." I stand behind the cash register excitedly. Simone never leaves the money drawer, she always makes sure to stand and keep an eye on the rustling coins and bills. "I'll replace you," I tell her quickly, not sure she heard me through the slamming door.

My fingers repeatedly polish the porcelain plates with the white cloth, arranging them in a pile, deciding to clean them again and placing them in a new stack.

Simone walks in and quietly closes the boulangerie door behind her, and I look up from the porcelain plates into her shining eyes as she approaches me and lowers her voice. "The BBC radio reported that the invasion has begun in Normandy. They said that the Americans and the British have taken over the coast."

My trembling hands keep wiping the plate I'm holding again and again. I'm thinking of the cannon battery in Normandy and the Polish soldier in German uniform holding flowers. Now they are shooting at Americans and British soldiers storming the barbed wire placed on the coast. Will they survive?

"Statue of Liberty, New York, America," I whisper.

"What did you say?" Simone asks.

"Nothing." I wipe away a tear.

***

Nemesis

August, 1944

Secret 8/2/1944

From: Western Front Wehrmacht Command

To: Army Group France

Subject: Preparations for the defense of Paris

Background: The U.S. Army has established units on Normandy's shores and is trying to break through the German defense line in order to occupy all of France and Paris.

General: French citizens should be treated as enemies rather than collaborators as in the past.

Tasks:

1. All Gestapo units and S.S. divisions should intimidate the civilian population in order to prevent insurgency and harm to German soldiers.

2. The Gestapo units will work to exterminate the resistance fighters without regard for innocent civilians.

3. All German female soldiers will be immediately evacuated from the Paris area in order to prevent the possibility of their capture.

SS. Telegram 483

The grey helmets will fight till the end

"Certificate, please." The German soldier standing in front of the guard post gives me a hostile look, keeping a safe distance, while his friend's submachine gun is aimed at my body.

"Guten morgen," I hand him my ID card and wait patiently. Although they see me every morning, they no longer smile as I pass their checkpoint on my way to work, crossing the wooden guard post and the barbed wire fences they have placed near the German Headquarters on Rivoli Street.

The soldier carefully examines the cardboard paper, looking at me and comparing my face to the photo attached, checking the stamps with his finger to make sure they are not fake.

"Monique Otin?"

Monique Moreno, I want to shout in his face that has almost disappeared under the grey metal helmet.

"Yes, it's me," I replace the shout with a polite smile.

"Have a nice day." He hands me the worn-out cardboard, returning to look at Concorde Square's wide roads, alert for a hidden enemy that might suddenly emerge.

I keep walking down the street and put the certificate back in my bag, not looking back. Since the invasion, I've been taking it out so often at the checkpoints all over the city that the cardboard has become faded, wrinkled under all those hands that examined it, and the eyes that stared at me.

A black car is coming towards me on Rivoli Street, and I stop walking, watching its silver lights aimed in my direction, getting closer.

"Guten morgen," I stop walking and say to a bored soldier standing next to one of the vehicles left in front of the headquarters.

"Bitte?"

"Do you have a light?" My hand searches for the cigarette pack in my bag while I turn my back to the black car as it slows down, and only the sound of the engine is heard on the empty street.

"Sure." He pulls out a metal army lighter, marked with the SS symbol, and I get close to his hand, smelling his scent of cologne mixed with grease.

"Thank you." I inhale the smoke. Did the car stop? I must continue walking. Otherwise he will start to suspect.

"Have a nice day." He returns the SS lighter to his pocket, and I have to keep on walking, my eyes following the small rear lights of the black car until it disappears around the corner. I'm safe this time.

I must not think about the horrible building at 84 Avenue Foch, but for a moment I have nausea, and I throw the unfinished cigarette into the street before I continue on my way, trying to breathe the clean morning air.

Above my head, I can hear the big red Nazi flag flying quietly in the morning breeze, as whispering above. Still, I look forward to the Louvre Palace, trying to count cars in front of the headquarters and getting away from the German soldier. Only a few of them left, and I do not know if they're all at the front or have started evacuating back to Germany.

A long convoy of trucks full of soldiers crosses the street on their way to the western front, in the direction of Normandy, and I follow them with my eyes, counting them and trying to identify the unit. The soldiers are crowded quietly and do not whistle in my direction, asking me to show them the city.

To my surprise, the boulangerie's front door is locked, and I have to walk by the alley around to the back door, stopping and looking over my shoulder to see if someone is following me. But Martin, the cook, is sitting inside his kingdom on an empty wooden crate, looking at the almost-empty pantry.

"She must have forgotten to open," he says, and I enter the boulangerie from the back.

At first I do not see her, but then I notice that Simone is bending behind the counter, opening the bottom drawer where we keep the tablecloths, pulling out a red-white-blue flag and kissing it carefully.

"You have arrived," she quickly turns as I place the bag on a chair.

"Good morning."

"It's just in case the Germans withdraw, but it's not going to happen." She hurries to return the flag to the bottom drawer and closes it.

"It's okay."

"Why didn't you enter from the front door?"

"It's okay. I will not say anything."

"I miss those days when women had values, and weren't peeking behind my back." She passes me, going to talk to Martin. I want to whisper in her ear that we are both on the same side, even if she is disgusted with me because I'm licking a German officer's boots, but I know she wouldn't believe me.

I also know she is listening to the BBC radio news, an offense worthy of execution by the black-coat Gestapo people. "I heard it from the neighbor," she tells me, but I do not believe her.

"Monique, Supply has not arrived again. You will have to go to the market and try to get some."

"Maybe Marie could go? I went yesterday and Tuesday."

"No, I want you to go. I do not trust her."

Despite my requests, she does not let me off the hook this time, and I get out and walk as fast as I can. I try to stay off the streets, and it's not just me; everyone is trying to avoid being outside while the Gestapo is searching for the resistance.

In the first days after the invasion, the city was waiting for the Americans to arrive, people made flags, and there were also brave ones who spat at German soldiers as they passed by. The German female soldiers, those who were called "grey mice" behind their backs, have completely disappeared from the city streets and are no longer seen walking down the Champs-Élysées holding cameras, as if they were on vacation.

But the days went by, and the German soldiers are still in the city, standing in the streets and checking people. What's going on at the front lines? Was the German counterattack successful, as the German army radio reported?

On the way to the market, I cross the newsstand, but even it can't tell me any news. The German army magazine and the daily newspaper are the only ones on display, yelling loud Nazi propaganda, which is limited to four thin sheets of paper.

"Papers, please." Two German soldiers are stopping people in the street, and I lower my eyes to their hobnail boots.

"Are you tense?"

"No, I'm not." I look at his dirty, greasy fingers.

"Bitte." He hands me back my papers, and I smile at him politely, walking as fast as I can, but there are three men in black coats near the market entrance.

"What took you so long?" Simone asks as I close the door behind me.

"The seller in the market said that since the invasion, there are barriers around the city. They are hardly letting supplies get in."

"And you brought nothing?"

"He said he didn't receive anything today."

"You should have argued with him."

"I did."

"You needed to do more. We do not have the privilege of not being loyal to the Germans and stopping providing them with what they want."

I look down and apologize, hurrying to put on my apron, and returning to the empty space behind the counter. Again I polish the porcelain plates and pray that it will all be over. Soon I'll hurry to the quiet apartment. Herr Ernest almost doesn't come anymore.

*   *   *

At first, when I close the thick wooden door behind me, hanging the bag by the apartment entrance, I do not notice anything unusual. But Oberst Ernest's voice from his study causes me to tense up, and I cross the hall into the living room and stand there.

The study door is open, and Herr Ernest sits in his leather chair, leaning in front of his documents and looking up at me like nothing has changed. Still, all the paintings on the walls, the ones we bought together, and others I have never seen, have been removed and concentrated at the side of the room, ready to be shipped. Besides the painting, there are several nailed wooden crates of wine and champagne, and maybe even cheeses and other foods that I cannot identify.

"Good afternoon, how are you?" He looks up from the documents in front of him but does not stand.

"I'm okay. How are you?" I stay at a safe distance from his study door.

"I'm fine, thank you, can you please make me something to drink?"

"Why are all the paintings off the walls?"

"I'm transferring them to the homeland," he says and returns to his writing.

"Why? I thought you were defeating the Americans."

Herr Ernest stops writing and looks at me.

"We are defeating them, and we are not preparing to leave Paris, certainly not without a German mark that will be remembered for eternity."

"What will you do to the city?"

"We will find a worthy solution for this city, just as the American bombers are destroying the cities of Germany."

"Are you going to destroy Paris?"

Herr Ernest examines me for a moment.

"I thought you were on our side."

"I'm on your side and think you'll stay here forever, so I do not understand why you're taking the paintings."

He raises his eyes again from the papers in front of him, and I fear that I've said too much, but he just smiles and goes back to reading.

"And what about my painting? The one I chose?" I can't stop myself, watching my dancer placed by the wall, near his hunters' paintings.

"Can you smell the fear of the people around us?" Herr Ernest raises his eyes from the document he is reading, looking at me with his green eyes. "I don't smell it anymore. Maybe it's time for a lesson about loyalty and betrayal, don't you think so?"

"I know I'm loyal to you," I place my trembling hands behind my back.

"I know you are loyal to the German nation and me. I was talking about the French nation and the price they are going to pay for their disloyalty." He smiles. "Why did you think I was talking about you?"

"Will you leave my painting here?" Is he trying to set me up?

"The painting must go to its new homeland. It is valuable. I cannot leave it behind. It is already German property. Please prepare a drink for me." He looks at me angrily.

For a moment, I want to ask him if I too am considered property for German use. Occupied property that will make its way into the thousand-year Reich's borders, but I prefer to look down and examine my painting, which lies by the wall. My dancer is still tying her ballet shoes, lying on her side, and it seems like her pink skirt is flying high, exposing her body to Herr Ernest's eyes if only he would look at her.

"Please leave the painting to me, just as I'm staying with you."

He looks at me in silence for a moment, as if debating whether to push me into the corner or let me go, at least for now, playing with me for his pleasure.

"I appreciate your loyalty and the remnants of German blood in your veins, but my dear, I'm the one who decides when you stop being with me."

The way he looks at me and says things makes me cringe, but I smile at him and keep holding my hands tight. I am his personal property, as long as he wants me.

"What would you like to drink?"

In the kitchen, I rest my hands on the sink, close my eyes, and take a few breaths. For a moment, I have a desire to open the knife drawer and examine its contents, but I stop myself and light a fire to heat the kettle. It's too dangerous to walk down the streets with a knife, especially now with all the surprise checks. I just have to stay alive, just a few more days, until the Americans succeed in breaking the German defense lines and come.

"After you're done with the coffee," his voice comes from the study,

"I'd be happy if you brushed my boots." I want them to shine for tomorrow morning.

Even though the window is open to the night air, I can't sleep beside Herr Ernest, and my eyes are fixed on the dark ceiling. I know I have to go to his study, but I can't. I'm too afraid, feeling stifled between the rooms and his shining hobnail boots guarding the entrance door, keeping me and my dancer painting from running away into the street.

***

The next morning, as I walk down the avenue, I see them emerge from a black car and stop in my place. I grip my handbag tightly in horror.

Like a black raptor, the vehicle arrives at a fast pace and stops next to a man walking in front of me down the street. He does not notice what is happening, continues to walk. And I want to shout at him to run away, but it is too late.

Three people in black coats jump out of the vehicle and grab him by force. Even though he tries to resist, they point a gun at his head and drag him into the car. In seconds, the doors are closed, and the vehicle continues to drive, disappearing behind the street corner.

Keep on walking, do not stop walking.

All the other people continue on their way as if nothing happened, turning their heads to the other side, only the ringing bell of the boulangerie door calms me down a bit. Here I'm a little safer.

"Monique, it's good that you're finally here. You're delayed just like all the farmers who are unable to supply flour."

I have no answer for her, and I hang my bag on the hanger, but it falls to the floor.

"What happened? Did you not sleep at night, that you have no strength?"

"I'm okay." I bend down to pick my bag from the floor with my shaking hand.

"So you'd better hurry, maybe some German soldier will come by chance and you can serve him."

"I'll be right there, I'm sorry." My fingers get tangled with tying the apron.

"Let me help you." She approaches me. "You are like the Americans. You need help with everything, unable to do anything properly. Is everything okay?"

"Yes, everything is fine."

"Do not cry. I did not mean what I said. It's just all this tension and the waiting for the Americans to arrive." She finishes apologizing and goes to the back room, probably scolding Marie.

When will the Gestapo arrive at my door? I try to make myself a cup of disgusting coffee substitute.

All morning the boulangerie
is empty, and I pass the time
listening to what Simone thinks
about the British and watching the
street, searching for black cars.
Still, by noon, I notice Violette
standing outside the glass door.

"Can I take a break?" I ask
Simone, already taking my apron
off.

"Did you hear? The Americans have
also invaded the south of France.
They conquered Nice." Violette
enters through the door. "They say
the German army is collapsing."

"Paris is not in the south of France,
and it has nothing to do with us,"
Simone answers her. But she too
is gripped by excitement. Without
noticing me standing next to her,

she bends down to the bottom drawer behind the counter, sliding her hand over the hidden flag, but quickly rises when she notices my gaze, wiping her face with her hand.

"Go, go. I need to re-fold the tablecloths," says Simone, "but don't stay outside for long, it is not safe anymore." And I hurry to remove my apron, going out into the summer sun outside.

"What is going to happen?" Violette asks in tears. "The Germans are retreating. They will not be able to protect Paris."

"No, they will not succeed, they will probably retreat soon."

"You promised me there would be no invasion and that the Germans would win."

"Yeah, I was wrong, I was wrong about so many things, I'm sorry."

We both stand on the Pont Des Arts, watching a group of German soldiers laying down sandbags on the bank, to the shouts of a nervous sergeant, preparing defensive positions for fighting throughout the city.

"Everything is falling apart, everything we had." She starts crying. "All I had."

"Do not worry, everything will return to normal." I watch the green water flowing leisurely. "We will continue to sit in cafés and drink fine coffee, strolling down the avenue." But deep inside, I know nothing will return to what it had been.

I had Dad and Mom and Jacob, who disappeared without me even being able to hug them one last time. How could everything go back to normal? I have nothing left, only Philip, who will never love me after what I did. And I don't even know if he is still alive or captured by the Gestapo. What world will I have after the Nazis go?

"At least you have your Fritz." I touch her hand for encouragement, but the touch is unpleasant for me, and after a moment, I return my hand to the metal railing. "Everything will be back to the way it was before the war, don't worry."

"Before the war, I was a simple girl without a spouse to walk with on the avenue." She continues to cry. "Even you have tears."

"Yes, even I have tears."

"See you tomorrow," I say goodbye to Simone. I have to hurry to the empty apartment, it is not safe in the streets, but the child is waiting for me by the newsstand. I have to go.

"Just a few more days." I kiss Violette on both cheeks. "Don't worry."

***

Just a Few More Days

"St. Joseph Street," the boy whispers to me, and I start walking. It is too dangerous to set a meeting point in the opera area. The place is full of Gestapo and people avoid entering the metro stations in the area.

But when I enter the quiet street, it is empty, and no one is waiting to accompany me, on foot or by bicycle.

"Get in the trunk of the van and wait," a man in work clothes passes by and whispers, disappearing behind the street corner and leaving me alone, watching the grey van parked and abandoned at the side of the alley. What's happening here?

As if by itself, my hand goes down
along my dress, looking for the
pocket, but there are no pockets in
this dress.

The street is quiet, and there is
no one around. Everything's okay.
I breathe quickly and enter the
trunk, closing the door behind
me, wrapping myself in darkness.
Breathe, everything's fine.

I can hear the car doors open and
close, and the engine starts, and
I breathe slowly, fighting the urge
not to open the door and escape.
I have done this before. I have to
trust them.

How long have we been going?
I've lost track of time. Are we still
in the city? The vehicle changes
direction every so often. We
are probably still in Paris. Is the

meeting at the place I met Philip for the first time? Will I meet him this time?

Suddenly the vehicle stops, and I tense.

"Shut off the engine," I hear a voice in German and want to scream.

***

"What?" I can hear a muffled sound.

"Shut down the engine," says the voice in bad French, and the monotonous engine rumbling stops. I must be quiet.

"Certificates, please." Rustling and then quiet.

"What do you have in the trunk?"

"It's empty. We're back from the market."

"Open the trunk."

Breathe, breathe, breathe, my nails scratch my thighs, breathe.

"No need, it's empty."

"Open it now." The voice in poor French is getting louder.

A barrage of gunshots, and footsteps, and more shots and a door slamming and shouting in German. My body is cramped in the dark as I bend my head and shove my fist into my mouth, stifling a scream.

"Run away." I hear a woman's shout, and another barrage of gunshots and my trembling hands grope for the trunk door handle in the dark, opening it and sending my legs out, stumbling for a moment on the road. The afternoon sunlight dazzles me, but I manage to stabilize myself and start running around the corner of a warehouse, running non-stop.

Run, run, run, do not look back.

My whole body hurts from the effort, the sweat, my heavy breathing. Keep running, another corner, hide behind it, now behind the hill, do not stop, ignore the pain of running, keep running, even further, between the bushes, do not stop running, further and further.

Only later, as I hide among the shrubs and try to catch my breath, I start to recall what my eyes had seen. The man in the black coat lying on the road in a strange position, looking at me with a hollow gaze as I burst out the back door and almost stumbled over him, the shouts in German that kept echoing in my head: "Shoot her, shoot her." And the strange, whistling noise passing me as I ran. What happened there? I have to hide and wait for the darkness. It doesn't matter what happened there.

The darkness is already falling when I dare to get out of my hiding place under a large bush, walking quietly on the path and listening. I have to keep walking. It did not happen to me, it happened to someone else, not to me. I was never there in the van.

My hips are scratched from the bushes, and I am already tired of walking. In what direction is the city? I must not be mistaken. Every time I see car lights approaching in the street, I hide until they pass. I walk through the abandoned warehouse area, hoping I'm going the right way, and the lights in the distance are directing me. I need to warn the man in the grey button-down shirt, something happened and I did not get to the meeting, he must know. There were other people there, and something happened to them too, what happened to them? I'll tell him.

I don't know what time it is when I reach the east bank, but it is clear that the curfew has already started and I must not be caught on the street.

Carefully I take off my shoes, ignoring the pain in my feet, and start walking barefoot so as not to make noise. Now and then, I hear the sounds of a German patrol's hobnails boots, and I hurry to hide in the alley or at the entrance to a stairwell, waiting for them to pass before I can continue walking. Was it planned? Did anyone betray us? I must know.

Near the apartment, the street is quiet. No car is waiting for me there, nor in the neighboring alleys, just a cool summer breeze and a single streetlight that shines dimly. Should I go upstairs? Are they waiting for me there? I have no other place to go, I must not stay in the street, it's too dangerous.

After waiting for long minutes in the stairwell, I carefully open the front door, afraid to enter, but the apartment is empty. No one is waiting to kill me as I scan the rooms in the dark, holding the kitchen knife tightly in my hand and moving suspiciously. I have to eat something.

My hands tremble as I struggle with the opener, unable to get it into the metal lid of the meat tin, trying again and again, opening it as much as I can and starting to hungrily swallow the greasy pulped meat. In the light of the candle, I notice the eagle stamped on the tin, its wings spread, and I remember the hollow look of the man in the black coat and the woman's shout: "Run away."

My legs no longer hold me up as

I collapse on the kitchen floor, vomiting, and starting to cry.

***

"You're late again. I will not give you extra privilege for living with the Germans." Simone raises her eyes from the money drawer the next morning when she hears the doorbell. But I can explain nothing to her. I cannot explain all the times I looked out the window last night, checking if a vehicle had arrived and people were coming to stand me by the wall. In the early morning hours, I woke up in a panic to loud noise, standing up, and noticing that the knife I'd held in my hand while sitting prepared at the chair in front of the entrance door had fallen out.

"I apologize. I will try to arrive on time." My hands take the apron from the hanger, tying it in mechanical motion. "What do you want me to do?"

"The usual, nothing has changed since yesterday."

"Yes, madame Simone." I will stand behind the counter as if nothing has changed from yesterday. What happened there?

I must meet and inform the man in the grey shirt that something happened. Are they looking for me, or was it a coincidence? Did I make a mistake, had they discovered my identity?

Some German pilots come in, pointing to the bread in silence and patiently waiting for me to pack it for them.

"Monique, you are not focused. They are in a hurry."

What could I have done that exposed me? Did Herr Ernest discover who I am, and sent his Gestapo dogs after me, wanting to hunt his French boot-licking mistress? My eyes rise, and I watch through the window, will a black car stop here in a few minutes?

"Four Reichsmark, please." I notice for the first time their buttoned grey uniforms, full of medals.

Did someone betray me? What does he know about me? My name? Does he know the name of Herr Ernest or the place where I work?

"Monique, they are waiting for the change."

"Danke." They thank me indifferently, slamming the door on their way out and causing me to tense from the noise.

"Monique, I need you to go to the market."

I'm too afraid to walk by myself, but I can't say 'no' to Simone. Slowly I take my bag and head out, closing the door behind me and scanning the street.

***

"It took you a while to visit me after the last dress you bought." Anaïs picks me up from Reception. "What happened? Do you need a new evening dress again?"

"I apologize. I was busy."

"You should buy one, the German ladies have stopped coming, they are scared, you will receive a big discount."

"I did not come to buy a new dress."

"So why did you come?" She takes out a cigarette and offers me one, but I refuse with a nervous smile, and she lights the cigarette for herself, inhaling the smoke with pleasure.

"So why did you come? Even cigarettes are hard to receive these days. Fritz stopped bringing me any."

"I came to ask how you are. I'll bring you cigarettes." I take the pack from my bag, offering it to her, but she refuses with a bitter smile.

"How am I? I'm fine, waiting for the Americans to come."

"And aren't you afraid?"

"What should I be afraid of?" She exhales the smoke into the air.

"The Germans, your Fritz, all this crazy war around us, the Americans."

"Anaïs knew how to get along with the Germans, and Anaïs will know how to get along with Americans," she answers indifferently and looks at me. "Are you scared?"

"Yes," I admit. "I'm afraid of everyone, of the Americans who want to kill us, of the Communists, of the Gestapo driving in the streets."

"You are the spouse of Oberst Ernest. You have nothing to fear from the Gestapo. As for everything else, we'll have to see." She smiles at me. "I'm sure the U.S. military has officers too."

Finally I say goodbye to her. She has to go back to work, and I have to go back to Simone, telling her that I couldn't find any butter at the market.

"See you soon," I say, but I'm not sure it's going to happen anymore. Soon they'll probably catch me.

On the way back, I hide every time a car passes on the street, waiting at a building entrance with my heart pounding. I have to relax.

"Revenge." The headline screams in black print on a poster pasted to a building wall on the street, and I slow down and try to read the text.

"They did a big operation yesterday, killing and capturing many of them." Two women whisper behind my back, and I keep standing, making myself continue to read the poster.

"Who? The Gestapo?" the other one asks.

"Yes, they say there was a traitor among them."

"May God protect the resistance. Let them survive," the other answers and crosses herself as they continue walking down the avenue, and I follow them with my eyes.

Philip, is he alive? I must know, I must talk to Lizette, she is the

only one that might know him.
And I start walking as fast as I can
to the metro station, forgetting
that the Gestapo is waiting at the
entrances, checking the passersby.

* * *

"Lizette, open up. It's me." I knock
hard on the door. I'd tried ringing
the bell for a long time, waiting
patiently and trying again before
knocking. But the door is still
closed. She does not usually go out
at such hours. "Lizette, open up.
It's me."

"She's not here." The neighbor
from next door opens her
apartment door, peeking out as if
ready to slam it at any moment.

"Excuse me, where is Lizette?"

"She's not here."

"Where is she? I must find her."

"Don't you know?"

"Know what?"

"Wait, aren't you the girl who lived here a year ago? I used to see you on the stairs, Monique?" She opens the door and approaches. "Don't you know?"

"Know what?"

"Lizette is gone, she was killed, the Gestapo killed her, the other neighbor said she tried to escape from a vehicle they'd stopped."

While running down the stairs, I can hear my pounding footsteps hitting the marble stairs as if drums were beating in my ears, and the neighbor's voice calling my name from a distance, but all there is are the drums in my head and the sharp metal sound of the building door when I burst into the street.

My hands grip my ears tightly as I bend down on my knees on the pavement, trying to silence the voices but failing. They do not stop, swirling loudly and making a strange whistle as they pass through my body. What did I do? Why is everyone dead instead of me? Even the embracing arm of the neighbor trying to hug me can't stop the screams, and I rise and run away from her, whispering to her as I get away: "Do not touch me, anyone who touches me dies."

The telegram

"Why did you light those candles?" Herr Ernest asks when we sit at the table.

"I thought there might be a blackout." I watch the four candles standing in the cabinet. Do the Christians light memory candles?

"Now blow them out. After we regroup north of Paris, there will be a lot of blackouts." He hungrily bites the canned meat I served.

"I thought you would stay with me forever." I rise from the chair and approach the candles, putting out the fire with my fingers, ignoring the heat and pain.

"We must retreat from Paris. There are traitors among the

French, passing information to our enemies. Return to your seat, aren't you hungry?"

"I'm not hungry today, I apologize. Would you like my meat?"

"But we are going to get revenge. They thought we wouldn't find them. We will catch them all. The ones that escaped, hiding in their holes like dirty rats. They won't stop us anymore. Is there wine left?"

"No, all the wine is gone. Is it okay if I go to sleep? I'm a little tired."

"Yes, you may. Thank you for a lovely dinner."

Later that night, with Herr Ernest beside me, I can't sleep. I feel the pain in my fingers and think about the man in uniform, the one in the silver-framed photo at Lizette's house, and I can't stop the tears.

Quietly I get out of bed and walk barefoot to the study.

Top Secret

8/16/1944

From: Division 44

To: Engineering brigade 7112

Subject: Preparations for destroying Paris monuments

1. 7112 Engineering Brigade will mark key sites and bridges in Paris prior to their demolition.

2. Maps and charts of the sites will be taken from the municipality of Paris.

3. Explosives will be supplied by Supply Battalion 4221, which is located at Le Bourget airport.

4. Destruction will take place after a direct order prior to retreating from Paris.

SS. Telegram 912

My eyes pass quickly over the telegram by candlelight, my fingers flipping through the other papers, searching and trying to read the most important ones before carefully putting them back in his leather bag, quietly returning to bed. What should I do with this information?

I must forget what I saw. The Americans are on the way. I just have to stay alive, wait for their arrival. I must not risk myself anymore. They are searching for me.

Even if I wanted to, I have no one to pass the information on to. I don't trust the man in the grey shirt with the buttons, and I can't find Philip.

My hand wipes the tears away in

the dark room while I constantly hear Herr Ernest's breathing beside me in bed. Soon the morning will come, and he will wake up.

I will pass the information in the diary on to someone. I don't know how, and I don't know to whom, but I will find a way.

The alarm clock rings early in the morning, and I sit up tense, hurrying to put on my silk robe and rushing to the kitchen to make him coffee, there is some left. But Herr Ernest gets dressed in silence and hurries out, leaving me alone in the kitchen in front of the boiling kettle. "Please don't come back,"

I whisper after I put my ear next to the wooden door, hearing the building's front door close behind him and going to get dressed. I have to hurry.

The boulevard is silent, and no German army vehicle crosses the road with rattling engine noise. Even the metro exit in the large square in front of the opera is empty of people. Only a few passersby stand and look at the posters hastily attached on the billboard during the night. "Popular uprising," shouts the headline. "The policemen and railway workers for Paris."

Another poster is calling for revolution, printed in black ink on the billboard.

"We are going to pay in blood

for this." One man expresses his opinion and makes room for me as I push between them, trying to read the rebels' instructions.

"They're already running away, like mice in their grey uniforms," says another, and I look around.

The magnificent café in front of the opera, which was always full of German soldiers, is closed, and no black-coat Gestapo is standing at the metro entrance. The streets are empty of Germans as if waiting for the change to come, but the Nazi flags still hang in front of the opera house, and as I hurry to the boulangerie I see two German armored vehicles passing by in the middle of the boulevard. The soldiers are standing alert, wearing round helmets and holding machine guns, ready for battle.

With a stone-cold stare, they watch the empty streets while driving slowly, making me stop and hide in one of the houses' entrances, feeling the rumble under my feet and waiting for them to disappear

'They will not run away like mice,' I whisper to myself and accelerate my steps. They are still here, and no one has yet been able to expel them, neither the Americans nor the resistance, not with any of the information I passed to Philip or his replacement.

The diary is at the bottom of my bag, and despite its light weight, I feel the leather strap cut into my shoulder, leaving a red mark on it, and I have to fight the urge to turn around and run away. I have to pass that information on. I owe it to Lizette.

Why did you kill her? I want to scream at the red flags hanging in front of the opera building, but even though the street is empty, I'm afraid someone will hear my cries.

Now Lizette is with the charming man who waited for her patiently, looking at her for so many years from the picture above the fireplace. She hugs him non-stop, wrapping him in her warm arms, as only she and Mom knew. I need to hurry, and I almost stumble because of my wet eyes.

Two more German armored vehicles in camouflage colors pass through the boulevard, their chains creaking noisily and the soldiers holding machine guns aimed at the sides of the street, the bullet chains ready to fire, waiting to send the copper bullets out on command. I must ignore them.

The newsstand is almost naked of all the newspapers that covered it in the past, exposing wooden boards carelessly painted in peeling colors. Only a simple government newspaper glorifying German victories is still for sale.

"I've run out of cigarettes," the salesman is looking to the sides, "even the simplest ones, try in a few days."

"I'm not searching for cigarettes. The boy, I need the kid."

"Which kid?"

"The boy with the grey cap, the one who is sometimes here and arranges the newspapers outside, at the back."

"I do not know such a boy."

"I need to find him. I have something for him."

"Mademoiselle, you have to go," he looks sideways apprehensively, examining whether I came alone and not calming down even when he notices no one is around.

"Please, I must find him. I know you can help me."

"He has disappeared, never come here again, ever." He lowers his gaze and turns to deal with his affairs, ignoring my presence. What to do?

"Please."

But he no longer answers me.

Simone rises towards me from behind the counter at the sound of the doorbell, but the boulangerie is quiet and dark, the wooden door to the back room is closed, and the trays in the display case, which were always full of pastries, are empty.

"Good morning." I gently close the door behind me.

"Good morning, Monique."

"What happened?" My eyes look around, trying to get used to the gloom.

"It is impossible to open today. We are closed."

"We are never closed."

"As of today we are closed, there were no groceries, and the market is closed, we can do nothing, we will have to wait until everything is over. Go home, I have already sent Martin and Marie away."

"What about you?"

"I will stay here, at least for now. I will wait for them here."

For a moment, she seems lonely to me in the dark boulangerie, and I would like to say something encouraging to her, but she never liked me too much.

"I'll help you arrange things, and then I'll go."

We both work side by side in silence, occasionally looking up the avenue at the sound of a German armored vehicle passing by in slow motion, shaking the road stones, and making us tense.

"What will you do when it's all over?" she asks me, taking the tablecloths out of the drawer and folding them again, even though there is no need.

"I don't longer believe it will end well."

"For women who collaborated horizontally, it will definitely not end well." She gives her opinion, and I know she means me. It doesn't matter anymore whether I live or not. What I did can no longer be changed.

"I have to go."

I quickly collect some leftover chocolate chip cookies. They are not fresh, but they are the last ones in the jar, and I have no other plans to pass on the information I have.

"When it's all over, if you want
to continue working here, you're
welcome," she says when I go to
open the door, probably for the last
time.

"Thanks." She does not really mean
it.

"Monique."

"Yes?"

"Be careful, take care of yourself."

With a slight slam, I close the door
behind me and hasten my steps
to the Latin Quarter, armed with
a diary full of crowded lines in my
handwriting and a paper bag of
chocolate cookies.

***

"What do you have in your bag?"

"A woman's belongings."

The soldier standing in front of the Pont Neuf Bridge military outpost looks at me indifferently while his friend examines my body with an eager look, moving his eyes from my dress to my feet. The policemen at the guard post have disappeared and been replaced by soldiers in grey and green uniforms, standing beside a machine gun position and barbed wire fences.

"Can I see the bag?"

"Please, it's for you." I take out the cigarette pack from the bottom of the bag, pull it out, and serve it to him.

"The whole pack?"

"The whole pack."

With a gesture, he puts the pack of cigarettes in his uniform pocket and instructs his friend to let me pass.

Don't look back, keep on walking, your eyes straight ahead, don't give him time to regret.

I ignore the soldiers measuring the bridge and the officer pointing with his finger, giving orders to a soldier who kneels at the bridge's center, painting white crosses on the old stones with a paintbrush.

Keep walking, enter the alley, only there will you feel safe. When I walk into the narrow street, I allow myself to stand for a few minutes and wipe my sweaty hand holding my bag and the diary inside.

The old alley walls are full of posters, urging citizens to revolt and take up arms. A few people gather around the entrance to a grocery store, talking to each other and pausing as I pass, scrutinizing me, reviewing my new dress.

I'm one of you, help me, I want to shout at them, but I know they will not believe me. Who will believe a young woman dressed elegantly in a poor neighborhood? After all, I cooperated horizontally with the Germans.

The basement entrance is also closed with a metal door, locked with a large padlock, and there is no one around to help me. Only the girl from the store smiles at me.

She looks at me with sparkling eyes through the old shop door, and I approach her hesitantly, wanting to give her the cookies I'd kept, especially for her.

"Get out of here," her mother whispers angrily, pulling her inside the store.

"I need you to help me." I follow her. I have no one else left.

"Get out of here and don't come back." She picks up a wooden stick.

"The man who was here a long time ago in the basement," I put the diary on the filthy counter. "Give this to him." And I turn my back and run away before she can say anything, before I regret it, before she looks at what is written inside and goes straight to the police or the Gestapo.

On the way back to the east bank,

I notice that I forgot to leave the bag of chocolate cookies for the girl, but I don't have the courage to return, and I sit on a bench, eating them and watching the Notre Dame Cathedral and the soldiers measuring the bridge. I have to talk to someone. I need to calm down.

"Anaïs no longer works here," the receptionist answers me with a smile of victory as I stand in front of her, asking to call her.

"What happened to her?"

"She did not come to work, disappeared, so she was fired. Can I help you with something else?"

"No, thank you, I was searching for Anaïs."

"If I were you, I wouldn't worry about her," she continues in her arrogant tone. When I go down the marble stairs, I think of Anaïs taking care of Anaïs, wondering which soldier her next occupation will be. With a perfect smile, she will show him all the treasures of Paris.

I can look for her at the apartment where she lives, she once told me the address, but I have a feeling she may not be there either, and worst of all, when I go down the street and start walking down the avenue towards the Lafayette Gallery, a few shots are heard.

A group of armed soldiers stands at the entrance to the big store, quickly running into battle positions, taking shelters behind the tree trunks. What should I do?

All the people disappeared from the street when the shouts began, leaving me standing alone on the sidewalk.

Where to run and hide? I manage to run to a nearby advertising column, bending and trembling at its feet. Who is shooting? All I can hear is the German shouts from the soldiers lying in the street. Where are the shots coming from?

Minutes pass on the street, no car passes, and only the sounds of tree branches in the wind is heard on the avenue.

"Everyone on your feet, keep on moving," the sergeant shouts in German at his soldiers, and they all rise and keep on marching down the street, looking around with weapons drawn and suspicious looks. As they pass by, I bury my head between my hands, cramped by the sound of their hobnails boots on the road.

"Are you okay? The danger is over. You can get up." A gentleman in a suit touches my shoulder and holds my hand, helping me up.

"Thanks." I look around, rubbing the dirt from the sidewalk off my knees. The soldiers have already moved further down the street.

"Go home. It is dangerous on the streets." He makes sure I'm fine before he walks away, and I hurry to the apartment. I have to stay there and wait. Soon everything will be over. Just a few more days.

***

Paris, Eighth arrondissement,

August 18, 1944 evening

All afternoon I am shut up at home, trying to read a book I took from the bookshelf, but I'm unable to concentrate, finding myself reading the same paragraph over and over again and losing concentration. Occasionally shots are heard through the open windows, making me cringe in the little living room armchair. What's going on outside?

The hot summer air penetrates the apartment, and only in the evening does a cool breeze enter. I peek out of the window and see people running, wondering if the Germans have abandoned the city, but a few minutes later a truck full of soldiers stops, and they quickly jump out of it, spreading in the street, causing me to withdraw from the window.

Have they come to arrest me? Did the woman in the store pass the diary I gave her to the Gestapo?

At first, as I'm trying to listen through the entrance door, the staircase is quiet. But suddenly I hear footsteps of hobnail boots climbing the wooden stairs, and I push my feet as hard as I can to block the door as they come. I will not give up without a fight.

"Monique? What are you doing?" I hear Herr Ernest from the other side of the thick door, trying to push it open.

"Sorry, I was scared. There were shots in the street today, I did not know if you would come back." I open the door slightly, trying to see if he's come alone.

"We evacuated the hotel. We're moving north, so I came to say goodbye." He stands in front of me, and I look up at him, checking his green eyes.

"You came to say goodbye?" Will I stay alive?

"Yes, I came to say goodbye, but before that, I have a few more things to finish here." He smiles at me, and I keep on smiling but want to scream.

"What kind of things?"

"Some orders that need to be executed tomorrow, and some things to check that they are done, not something that should interest a pleasant companion like you."

"Is it related to Paris?"

"It has to do with German honor," he answers flatly, removing his military shirt and draping it on the arm of the chair, exposing his pale body while remaining in only a sweaty green tanktop. "We will leave after giving the French nation a present, the same we gave the Communists and the Jews. We will always destroy the ones trying to fight and betray us." He keeps talking, but it seems he is mostly talking to himself as he organizes the few things left in his study, turning his back and ignoring my presence.

"What do you mean? Is it about all the stories coming from the east?" I stand outside the study door and ask, regretting it a moment later.

Herr Ernest stops arranging the papers on his desk and looks at me.

"You think the German army is losing, but we never lose. You just don't know how to view history. The Communists and the Jews did not defeat us. Like rats, they entered the camps we built for them."

"What camps?" I lower my eyes, unable to look at his fingers holding the telegrams and commands.

"What does the name matter? Camps we built to ensure German supremacy against the Jews and their ambitions to rule the world."

My fingers scratch the doorframe of his study, but he continues.

"One day you will all thank us for what we did. Please make me dinner."

We eat dinner in silence, and after that he continues to work, leaving me to nap in the small armchair until the door opens, and he goes to bed, not before he sets the alarm clock next to his dresser.

"What happens tomorrow? When are you going back to the army?"

"Tomorrow morning, we will say goodbye properly." He smiles and sits down on the bed, removing his tank top and lying down to sleep.

I cannot go to bed with him, but I must, otherwise he will suspect me.

***

The city is quiet in the dark, and the gunfire sounds have ceased, but I cannot fall asleep. My eyes look at the bedroom curtain moving gently in the night breeze, and I think about Auschwitz in the east that he built for my family.

The streetlights are almost all off, and the city outside is dark, as if waiting for tomorrow. What did he write in the study? The pain in my stomach does not stop.

Even though I have no one to pass the information on to, I can't help myself, and I rise quietly, walking barefoot to the study door, gently closing it behind my back and sitting in his chair.

Top Secret 8/19/1944

From: Engineering brigade 7112, Commander

To: Engineering brigade 7112 Units

Subject: Destroying Paris monuments

Commencement of operations, starting at 8/20/1944 08:00 after the departure of the main army units from the city, executing according to plan.

Oberst Ernest

7112, Commander

My eyes quickly go through the destruction order he has already signed, examining his signature at the bottom of the page, and the pain in my stomach intensifies. What to do?

I must hurry, my hands moving quickly between the documents, and my hand accidentally hits his fountain pen's ink jar lying on the side of the table.

Even though I try to catch it, the ink jar slips through my fingers and hits the wooden floor, crashing into sharp pieces of glass that sound like they're shaking the whole apartment.

I freeze in place. What have I done? Did he wake up?

"I'm dead," my lips whisper again and again as I get down on my knees, trying to stop the ink stain from spreading on the floor, moving my fingers quickly around the black liquid, which looks like a stain of dark blood expanding without stopping.

"What have I done?" I speak to myself, ignoring the small pieces of glass scattered on the floor that wound my hands, making me bleed on the parquet, dotting the wood with burgundy spots in the dim light of the candle.

I'm dead. The dark stain has been absorbed into the wooden boards and spreads to the carpet, painting its edges black, which my ink-soiled fingers fail to scratch away. Soon he will wake up and kill me, what will I tell him? I will no longer be alive when the Americans arrive.

The hours pass as I kneel on the rug, hugging myself and holding my aching stomach tightly, ignoring the blood and black paint on my hands, soiling my nightgown, painting it with stains. Soon, before sunrise, the bedside clock will ring shrilly, and he will wake up, get out of bed, come looking for me. I will no longer get to see the morning sun.

What was Lizette doing?

In a quick motion, I get up from the ink-stained carpet and walk out of his study, closing the door behind me as quietly as I can and stepping into the dark kitchen. My hands search for the drawer, and my wounded fingers hold the wooden handle firmly. I'm dead anyway.

Do not stop and think, do not hesitate, walk to the bedroom, be careful in the dark, do not stumble and make noise. I can see Herr Ernest lying under the blanket, and I raise my hand above my head, holding the handle firmly until my fingers turn white.

"You murdered my father!" I shout, and lower the knife with all my might, pushing it firmly against his twisting body, hearing him scream in pain.

"You murdered my mother!" I shout again as the knife goes down once more, but then I feel his hand hit me in the chest, and my breathing stops as his fingers grope upwards, searching for my neck.

"You..." I try to slam the knife into his body again, but his fingers close tightly around my neck, and he squeezes and squeezes, trying to rise above me.

"Traitor," I hear him whisper as he tightens the grip of his fingers.

Breathe, breathe. I'm choking and trying to release his grip on my neck. I can't see anything. He is strangling me. Where's the knife? I must hit him again with the knife. Where did the knife go?

"Dirty Frenchwoman," he says hoarsely, squeezing my neck and hitting my chest. My hand searches for the knife on the sheets. Where is it? What is all that wetness?

"You will die like everyone else," I hear his whisper close to me. Air, I need air. My hand slips on his suffocating fingers, trying to remove them with all my might.

He's too strong. I'm not succeeding. Air, I have to breathe. The knife, here it is. I feel it in the palm of my other hand, grab it again, and continue to strike him. He does not let go. I need air, please. I must breathe. I'm suffocating but stabbing him again and again. I want to live.

I gasp. A drop of air, he is losing his grip a bit. I need air. I cough and try to push him off me. He is so heavy, and what's that wetness? Everything is wet. Do not stop stabbing, stabbing, stabbing.

Release me already!

My free hand slips again on his fingers that grip my neck, and I manage to pry them slightly. Air.

"You killed my Jacob!" I manage to scream hoarsely, and push him away from me with all my might, coughing from the effort and trying to breathe again.

"You murdered my Lizette!" I shout at him in a distorted voice and lower the knife as hard as I can.

"I'm Monique Moreno, and I'm a French Jew!" I scream with all my might as I cough and pant, lowering the knife one last time into his twisted, quiet body, throwing it away, and running out of the room.

***

Paris, Eighth arrondissement,

August 19, 1944, early morning

When will he wake up and kill me?

I do not know how long I have been in the bathroom, curled up on the floor, waiting to hear the gunshot. My eyes close when I imagine Herr Ernest getting up out of my bed, crawling to his study where his firearm is waiting for him in the black leather case, and coming to hunt me in the bathroom. I'm too afraid to open my eyes.

The alarm clock starts ringing with a loud whirring, and my whole body cramps in fear as I cuddle my legs tightly.

"Please stop, please stop," I whispered to the clock, closing my eyes, but it rings for more and more long minutes until it stops.

And the house is quiet again.

The morning's twilight has painted the house in blue, and I open my eyes and examine myself, looking at my hands in disgust and nausea. My fingers are painted with clotted blood mixed with black ink stains, and I have to fight the urge to vomit. I have to grip the sink as I get up and stand, trying to wash and scrub my hands and skin until they become red and sore, splashing water on the nightgown to clean it as well. But I'm not going to my bedroom to change into a dress. He's probably waiting for me, awake, hiding behind the door and waiting to kill me.

But he does not come out of my bedroom.

As the day goes by, I can hear the shots from the open windows, sometimes the sounds are distant, and one time a fight takes place on the street below. The bullets hit the building walls, scattering shards and causing me to crawl on the floor near the sink.

"They're on their way," I whisper when the phone in his study rings and does not stop, but I do not dare to approach and answer. He is waiting to kill me.

Soon they will reach me. Towards noon, I crawl to the front door, kneeling on the floor and listening through the heavy door to the voices on the staircase. Despite the wooden table I dragged against the door. I know that even if I try my best, they will break it easily if they arrive. They will put me in front of the wall and shoot me. This time it will be my turn, and I watch his hobnails boots that are standing by the door, prepared to hit me in the name of their master.

Shouts in German are heard in the street, followed by gunfire. Without thinking, I get up and run to the kitchen, trying to find a hiding place.

Holding a knife, I try to loosen the pantry boards, but the panels do not come loose and the knife slips, scratching my hand and making me scream in pain. I'm too scared to hide in the bedroom closet. He's in the room, waiting for me.

Crawling, I return to my hiding

place under the sink, holding
my wounded hand and trying to
prevent the blood from dripping,
this is the safest place to spend the
night until they come to pick me
up.

"I'm Monique Moreno, I'm Monique
Moreno," I whisper to myself over
and over as it gets dark outside. I
must not fall asleep, but my eyes
are closing, I can no longer hold
them open.

***

"Where am I?"

My whole body aches from lying
on the bathroom floor as I get up
quickly. The house is still quiet.

Morning daylight illuminates the house from the open windows, and the sounds of gunfire are heard from time to time. I must get away from this apartment, it's dangerous for me.

Carefully I enter my bedroom, looking at the wall, and ignoring the crimson stain that paints the blanket and what is underneath it. Walking in small steps, my back to the bed, concentrating only on the closet door, I open it, choosing the first simple dress I lay my hands on, and quickly run out of the room, breathing again only when I'm outside.

What to take with me? I need some food. I haven't eaten anything since yesterday, my hands move quickly between the pantry shelves, putting a chocolate bar into my dress pocket. The thought of him lying in the other room makes me nauseous, and I grab the wooden shelf to stabilize myself. I have to hurry. What about his gun? The leather case hangs in his study. Shall I take his gun? I do not know how to use it, but I can threaten if I have to. Slowly, I pull the handgun out of the holster, surprised by the metal's oily touch, and put it in my bag.

Anxiously I get closer to his dirty hobnail boots, kicking them as hard as I can, and I open the front door. The stairwell is empty, and I hurry out of the apartment, going down the stairs out to the street.

The intense light outside is bright in my eyes when I open the building's front door, and I have to wait a few seconds at the entrance hall and watch outside, getting used to the sun.

A German military staff vehicle stands abandoned near the building entrance, its tires punctured, its upholstery torn. Is this the vehicle I'd been inside so many times? Several people pass me running, and I start to follow them. But then I stop and look at the black vehicle waiting for me at the end of the street.

The black car stands across the street as if trying to block it, with its doors open, waiting to put me inside and take me to the horrible building at 84 Avenue Foch. What to do?

I hear a series of shots from the other side of the block, and I cringe in place. What direction to go? Will they shoot me if I start running? The person standing next to the car is not looking in my direction, and I slowly approach the black vehicle, ready to turn around and run.

One man in a black leather coat lies on the street corner, his face to the pavement, and a wet stain of crimson surrounds him, while another man sits by the wheel, leaning on it as though sleeping between the shattered windows and the bullet holes in the dark doors and seats.

Keep on walking with the people towards the boulevard, get away from the black vehicle, assimilate among them, do not stop, and look at the tricolor flag placed on the black car's hood. Just keep walking.

Near the Champs-Élysées, there are more people and more shouts, some citizens waving guns in their hands, some holding the flag of free France, but in every direction shots are heard, and the crowd is running to take shelter behind tree trunks or advertising columns in the street.

I'm saved. I'm one of them, one anonymous girl in the crowd. I survived, I survived.

***

Paris, Eighth arrondissement,

20 August 1944 10:30 AM

"She's German. She's a collaborator." There is a shout in the crowd, and I look around to see who they mean.

"That's her, in the brown dress." I can hear the scream again, and some people stop and look at me. I have to keep walking.

"She licked a German officer's boots," the woman continues to shout, and the people start surrounding me until I have no choice but to stop and turn around, facing the neighbor from the third floor below my apartment. She is standing and pointing at me with a look full of hatred.

"She's a collaborator."

"It's not true. I'm French, like you."

"She's German." And more people crowd around with murmurs of rage.

"It's not true."

"She's in love with a Nazi officer," she shouts, and I feel a thump in my back and fold, almost falling to the ground.

"I'm French."

"Her officer housed her in a Jewish family's apartment. She collaborates horizontally," she shouts to the crowd.

"Please, it's not true." I try to run, but they stop me, and another fist is thrown at my stomach, and hands grip me tightly.

"Look what I found in her pocket." There is a roar of joy when a young man pulls out the package of chocolates and presents it over his head, showing the audience around him the cover with the eagle holding a swastika under the word 'chocolate' in German. "Only the Nazis have such delicacies." And the crowd murmurs in agreement, and I feel spit hitting my face, followed by a kick in my stomach and slaps that send me to the ground.

"Kill the horizontal collaborator."

"Kill her."

"Bullet to her head."

"Please, I'm French." I try to get up and protect my face from the kicks and spitting. "Please."

The gun in the bag, it will protect me, I have to live, please. But my hands looking for my bag on the sidewalk can't find it between the shoes of strangers trying to kick me. I've lost my bag. It fell or was snatched from me by someone in the crowd. I want to live so much.

"We will give her the special collaborators treatment," someone suggests and grabs me by the arm, dragging me down the avenue to the cheers of the crowd that surrounds me, still cursing and spitting in my face.

"Take care of her."

"Engrave a swastika on her cheeks."

"Cut off her hair that everyone knows."

"I've brought you another one."
He throws me into the center
of a crowd where several other
young women are standing in torn
dresses, eyes downcast.

"Another one," cheers the crowd,
"we'll take care of them all." And
through my tears, I see Violette in
the center of the circle.

Two men force her to sit on a chair
taken out to the street from one of
the cafés, a sturdy guy is holding
her while another in a white
tanktop cuts all her hair off with
scissors. The crowd is shouting
and cursing her, cheering on every
clump of hair thrown into the
street.

"Make her a beautiful bald spot."

"Let everyone know what she was
doing."

"Do not forget a swastika on the forehead, she will be beautiful."

I cannot look at her like that, and I lower my eyes. Maybe it's better that I'm shedding so many tears and everything is blurred. Why is this happening to me?

"You're next in line." The man tightly holding me whispers as Violette is lifted from the chair and led to a display in front of the bloodthirsty crowd.

"Please, this is a mistake."

"Shut up." He slaps and kicks me again, and I stumble and fall on the sidewalk, trying to stabilize myself and holding the pavement stones with my fingers and fingernails.

A huge hand grabs my hair and

lifts me to a standing position, and I scream in pain as he presses me to his body. He is a big man, really big, sweaty, wearing a grey tank top full of stains and smelling of sauerkraut, wearing a filthy beret, and his eyes look at the crowd angrily.

"She is Jewish, no one touches her."

"She collaborated horizontally." Voices from the crowd answer him as he begins to drag me out of the circle.

"She's German. We'll take care of her," says a man who tries to grab my arm.

"No one comes near her." I hear his thunderous voice above the roars of the crowd as he presses me close to his body with his huge hand, and I notice the resistance armband around his thick arm.

"She licked German boots." Another young man tries to get closer to me, but the huge man pushes him away.

"Do not touch her."

"There are no Jews in France, the Germans killed them all. She belongs to us." The young man does not give up as the crowd closes on us.

"Anyone who gets closer will die," the big man shouts and points his rifle at the young man, hugging me with his other arm. And the young man stops and steps back, not before spitting on me, turning to the next young woman waiting for her punishment in a torn dress and with a downcast look.

"Give her to him. We have enough horizontal collaborators."

"We must hurry." He supports and drags me, pushing the crowd to the sides by force and carrying me between the people gathering around the young woman who is forcibly seated in the chair in the middle of the street.

"Run." That's all he says, and we start running down the boulevard. I'm running as fast as I can, getting away from the crowd before anyone else tries to hit me. The pain in my ribs from the kicks does not stop, and it is difficult for me to breathe. Still, I keep running, ignoring the sounds of shooting all around and trying to be careful that my shoes do not fall off while running, but after a while I have to stop. I can't breathe anymore.

"We must go on." He encourages me and holds my hand, does not allow me to stop, but he too is gasping and goes for a walk as we approach Concorde Square.

I'm trying to catch my breath, ignoring the pain in my ribs and my torn and filthy dress. His sweaty hand supports my body as he leads me behind a burned-out car parked on the side of the boulevard. There is gunfire all around, and we have to lower our heads.

I cannot run anymore. The smell of the burnt vehicle penetrates my nostrils and fills them with a pungent smell, mixed with my heavy breathing and my sweat.

"I've been looking for you for three days," he says.

***

"Who's looking for me?" My voice sounds hoarse, like someone else's. I'm gasping for air, tensing up every time a shot is fired from the direction of Rivoli Street, unable to raise my head.

"They are looking after you," he answers and puts his arm around me to protect me, wrapping me in the smell of sauerkraut while I hold my head tightly between my two hands and try to bury myself in the road, wanting to escape from the round of shots in the square. Who is looking after me? Who cares about me? I'm just trying to breathe and stay alive in all the gunfire surrounding us. I'm so tired of being afraid.

Some people are running hunched towards the barriers and barbed wire fences in the square's center, holding rifles in their hands, but the shots are getting heavier, and their bodies suddenly fold and remain lying on the road. "I can't anymore," I scream and bury my head in his big hand.

"We have to move towards the street."

In front of the Nazi headquarters on Rivoli Street, several German cars are burning, raising black smoke to the sky. Occasionally, an orange flash of an ammunition explosion hits one of them, and the fire lights up again, causing me to tremble and scratch the road.

"I can't."

"You must."

Down the street, there are two German armored vehicles firing machine guns in our direction, and bullets are pounding on the buildings around the square, leaving holes in them, but the huge red Nazi flag in front of the headquarters is thrown onto the street.

"I can't."

"Run." He gets up and pulls me, forcing me to run next to him, and we skip and try to cross the square and reach the garden area, passing the sign at the gate which is punched through with bullet holes, kneeling next to a stone shelter, catching our breath.

"I can't anymore."

"We have to get to the Louvre and cross the river. The Latin Quarter is already ours." He gasps as we look around carefully.

A German vehicle enters the square, driving fast and turning around the fountain, and the big man picks up his rifle and tries to shoot at it, but the vehicle manages to escape towards the bridge while I cringe from the gunfire, holding the big man's legs tightly.

"We're trying to stop them from getting to the bridges. They have a plan to blow them up, but they're delaying. It's not clear why," he yells at me even though we're close to each other.

We hear a burst of gunfire, followed by an engine's rumble and creaking chains around the corner, and the noise gets louder.

"Run," he yells, and we get up together as he takes my hand and

pulls me after him towards the
garden and the river.

* * *

The sounds of gunfire never stop.
Even as we approach the river,
we hear the whistling of bullets
and the rumble of machine guns
from the direction of Île de la
Cité. But the river flows leisurely,
its waters greenish in the midday
sun, moving slowly and calmly,
indifferent to the sounds of gunfire
all around as if it does not care
at all about the war taking place
in the city. The Pont Des Arts
stretches peacefully from side to
side, empty of people with only the
lanterns along it seeming to me
like people walking on it.

"Germans," the big man in the stained shirt whispers and points with his finger at the camouflaged position and the round grey helmets that reflect the August sun, and I feel I can no longer move. They are going to kill us.

"Wait for me here," he whispers, but I grab his filthy shirt and move with him, even though I'm probably hampering his movement. I close my eyes tightly as he lifts his rifle and aims, and my hand squeezes his shirt with each shot fired at the German soldiers.

"Run," he yells at me as he starts running towards the bridge.

"I can't. They will kill me."

"Come with me." He turns around and pulls me, lifts me to my feet, and we start running.

Do not stop running, ignore the
soldiers lying in strange positions
behind the sandbags, be careful
not to stumble on the wide stairs
that climb to the bridge, ignore the
pain, look forward to the other side
of the bridge. Do not stop running.

The sound of my breathing fills all
my thoughts, and the bridge is not
ending. I feel so exposed as the
big man runs beside me, grabs
his rifle, with two more rifles from
the German position on his back.
Another step, and another, and
I can hear the strange whistles
in my ears. The other side is so
close, but suddenly the big man
folds and falls on the bridge while
I'm screaming and stopping next
to him, trying to drag him off the
bridge. But he is so heavy, and
I'm small, and a puddle of blood
appears under his body, and I keep

hearing the strange whistles all around us, cutting the air around me and the bullets splitting the wooden boards of the bridge as they penetrate. Suddenly the end of the bridge seems so far away.

"Hold on," I keep screaming at him, "we will soon arrive." I turn him on his back and rip the remnants of the pocket from my dress, shoving it where the blood is coming out and trying to drag him onto the wooden boards which are full of bullet holes, and someone comes from the other bank, yelling at me to keep running. And all I do is grab the big man's hand and shout: "Help me carry him, help me carry him."

***

Paris, Barricade near Pont Des Arts, August 20, 1944, 12:30 PM

Philip

"Philip, I have two more volunteers. Where should I send them?"

Since the Gestapo raid, we have had a shortage of people, they managed to penetrate so deeply, and now we are already past twenty-four hours of fighting all over the city. The police headquarters in Île de la Cité is already ours, but the people there are besieged, and ammunition is running low.

"Do you have any more resistance armbands?"

"Yes, I do."

"Give them to the new ones and take them to the barricade in the direction of the invalid. They have a shortage of fighters. See if you have some guns to give them."

Since the Gestapo raid, the connection between the members has been severed, even with her, and I have no idea if she is still alive. The chances are that the Gestapo got her. I'm trying not to think about it, even though it's so hard.

"Philip, we got another German machine gun. Where should we place it?"

"Take it to Saint-Michel, tell them to try to pass it to the fighters at Île de la Cité."

"Shouldn't we try to overcome the German snipers firing at us from the Louvre?"

"No, we'll get along here. They're in trouble there."

"Philip, we are receiving information from Versailles that they can hear the American tanks."

"Pass that information to all commanders, tell them they have to hold on for a few more hours."

It is my fault. I led her to the traitor. He must have managed to get enough information out of her. Even though he is dead now, it doesn't make me feel better. Lizette was killed, and the newspaper boy was killed, and they probably killed her too.

"Did you hear anything from the Breton?"

"No, should I replace you here? You've been in position since yesterday."

"No, I'll be here a little longer."

Since the first time I saw her, I wanted to know her better. She was standing scared in front of me, in that old warehouse, afraid but willing to fight for her life. Every time we met, I adored her outbursts of anger, saying what she thought and not what I wanted to hear. But she did not want to see me, and now it probably does not matter anymore.

"Philip, they're running out of ammunition at the barricade in front of Luxembourg Palace."

"They'll have to settle with what they have for now, I'll try to arrange more."

Only her diary arrived somehow.
Apparently it's hers, I'm not
even sure of that. How much of
her handwriting had I seen? I
always told her to be careful. One
woman from an alley shop in the
Latin Quarter passed the diary
to someone who passed it on to
someone, and he came to us. Since
then, we have been lurking near
the bridges, hitting the Germans
when they try to get closer. But she
just disappeared.

"Are you sure no one has heard
anything from the Breton?"

"I'm sure. I also checked on the
positions in San Michelle."

Only the man from the market,
the giant Breton, might be able to
recognize her. He is the only one
who knows her and is still alive. He

volunteered to search for her, but he has been wandering on the east bank for several days now.

"Philip, pay attention, there are shots from the Louvre area, near the German position."

"Bring the machine gun that controls the river here. I want you to place it next to me."

A few gunshots stop for a moment as we tense and examine the other bank, and suddenly two people climb on the bridge and start running towards us, and the fighter next to me asks whether to shoot them or not. I tell him to wait, and the German soldiers in the Louvre start firing at them, and I shout for them to bring the machine gun to start returning fire towards the windows and the

Germans. The people running towards us are already at the center of the bridge, one big and one smaller, probably a woman. It seems like they're advancing so slowly, and the big one suddenly falls, as he's been hit. The woman turns and stops next to him and leans over. She might have been hit as well. I can see the gunshots around them on the bridge, and I yell at the fighters next to me to start firing at the windows with everything they have. I jump over the barricade and run towards the bridge. It seems that another one or two are running after me, and I hear the whistle of the bullets as I approach, shouting for the woman to leave him and keep on running to the bank. Her hands are full of blood as she tries to drag the big man lying on the wooden bridge, and she doesn't stop yelling at me: "Help me carry him, help me carry him."

***

The Bridge

Monique

"Let me help you." I hear him, but my eyes are focused on the wooden boards on the bridge, seeing the bullets make holes that damage the wood, and small chips splash into the air. I look up for a moment and stare at his face.

He has not changed much. But he looks more tired and unshaven, and the smell of gun oil on his fingers is stronger too. He smiles at me for a moment and releases my fingers from the arm of the big man lying on the bridge.

"Philip!" I shout at him.

"It's okay. I'll take him. Keep running to the bank." He yells back at me, trying to overcome the surrounding noise of all the explosions and whistles, and I concentrate only on him and his brown jacket, moving as if in slow motion with every movement of his body.

But before I can answer him, he turns his back on me and leans over to the big man, bending over and loading him onto his shoulder. The big man's arms are moving like a rag doll's.

"Philip!" I get up and shout at him, but for some reason my voice comes out in a whisper, and only the whistles of the bullets do not stop.

"Philip, I love you..." I shout at him again, but he is already walking away from me with the wounded man on his shoulder, not noticing me, and again I whisper, and I feel the taste of blood in my mouth. It's probably from my hands, trying to take care of the big man. When did I touch them with my mouth?

"Philip..." He does not hear me at all, and I try to follow him towards the bank. I will tell him that I have been looking for him for so long, and that I hope he will forgive me for everything I did, and for being with a German officer, and that I love him so much. But he keeps moving away from me in a slow run, with the big man loaded on his back. Only two or three more people are on the bridge. I don't know exactly how many, and they all have resistance bands on their arms, and they stand and shoot. I'll go after him. He must listen to me.

"Philip!" I manage to shout, even though I cannot hear myself. Everything in my mouth is just the taste of blood, and I walk a few steps and for some reason fall, and it does not hurt me at all.

"Bend down," one of the people on the bridge shouts at me, not stopping to shoot, and the hoarse sound of the bullets continues around me. I see the ammo cartridges bouncing off his weapon and scattering around me.

"I have to tell him I love him," I whisper to the wooden boards on the bridge.

"You were injured, do not move." I think someone is yelling at me, but I'm not sure anymore. Maybe he's confused, maybe he's yelling to someone else, and I think he's putting his hand on my shoulder or grabbing me and starting to carry me. All around there are such strange whistles and blood. Where does this taste of blood come from?

"Philip, I love you," I whisper, but I do not think anyone hears me at all.

And suddenly everything is dark and so quiet.

Quiet.

****

Backroom of the Paris municipality, two years later.

"Is the dress nice?" I look at her.

"Your dress is beautiful, and you're so lovely." She smiles at me and hugs me tightly, wrapping her hands around my shoulders, calming me down. I have to relax.

"You look wonderful," she says, taking a few steps back and examining me, and I smile back at her, really hoping she's right. I'm no longer afraid of that she will hit me with that wooden stick she keeps behind the counter in the small shop she runs alone in the Latin Quarter.

"I have a surprise for you," she

whispers to me. "I managed to get back the diary you put on the counter in my shop, that time in the Latin Quarter, even though it is a bit ruined." And she puts the diary in my hand, with the name 'Monique' engraved on its cover in rounded letters. I'm holding it gently in my hands, flipping through the pages, and I start crying, remembering the diary I'd buried in the street that awful day I ran away.

I could not find that diary. As much as I tried to search the streets, I could not remember the exact place where I'd hidden it, and the diary remained buried under the pavement in the Marais district, bearing the dedication: "With love, Mom and Dad."

"I apologize. I did not mean to upset you," she hugs me. "I'll help you wipe away the tears. You mustn't cry and ruin your makeup."

 "Mom, she's the most beautiful princess in the world," Juliette, her daughter, whispers to her. She used to take the meat boxes from my hands and run away, and now she wears a floral dress with a pink ribbon on her head, walking excitedly non-stop in the small room, holding a bouquet of roses tightly in her hands.

Has he arrived? Is he waiting for me? Should I go out already?

"Monique, you're so beautiful, but hold up your chin." Mrs. Simone enters the room, elegantly dressed, and looks at me. After a moment, she turns her back on me and seems to be wiping away a tear.

"Did they arrive?" I ask her. Will everyone look at me?

"Just a few people, do not worry." She turns to me and waves her hand, dismissing my fears, and does not hold back, and hugs me. "Don't worry," she whispers to me. "We're all with you."

"Monique, are you ready?" The big man walks through the door.

"Close the door. He must not see her," Mrs. Simone scolds him, and he smiles at her and then at me. He wears a clean shirt and a suit and even a tie, and he has no smell of sauerkraut anymore. He approaches me and quietly asks: "Are you ready?"

"I'm ready," I whisper to him as he holds my arm, and the women rush out of the small room, leaving only Juliette with us.

I am scared. Will he always love me the way I love him?

"It's time," the big man smiles at me, and we walk through the door.

The great hall, which was empty when we arrived earlier, is now full of people who fall silent at once as we go inside and start walking down the aisle, and in the quiet of the hall I can hear the footsteps of Juliette's shoes behind me.

Of all the people staring at me, it seems that I can see Martin the cook standing and smiling at me, and Mrs. Simone wiping away a tear, and distant relatives of Mom and Dad as well. But Mom and

Dad and Jacob are not here, and the tears are streaming down my cheeks. And the hall full of people, most of them I do not know. I think they were part of the Resistance during the war.

As I look to the other side, it seems to me that maybe I notice Anais standing at the far end of the room, by the entrance door, next to a businessman in a respectable suit, but I'm not sure. The tears make it difficult to me to see, and so is the veil.

"They look at me because I'm limping," I whisper, and cling to the big man, trying to draw confidence from his hand holding me.

"They're looking at you because you're wearing a white dress," he whispers back and continues to lead me down the aisle towards the man waiting for me.

Philip stands at the end of the room in a suit he has agreed to wear especially for the occasion, but his quiff remains wild as if refusing to subject itself to conventions and status. His smiling gaze is focused only on me, walking slowly towards him.

"I've been waiting a long time for you," he holds my hand and whispers to me as I stand in front of him.

"I arrived as quickly as I could." I smile at him and press my lips to his, ignoring the town clerk who is waiting patiently to marry us.

***

In memory of all the Jews of France who perished in the Holocaust

In memory of all the resistance members who fought against the Germans, the few against many.

The End

Author's note: Pieces of History

When I started writing this book,
I knew I would write about
an emotional period for the
French nation: days of living,
collaborating, and resistance under
German occupation in World War
II, and above all, the help given to
the Nazis to capture the Jews and
send them for extermination.

Operation Spring Breeze,
mentioned at the beginning of
this book, is the first step of Paris'
Jewish deportation. During the
surprise operation that on July 16,
1942, the Paris police carried out
the capture of Parisian Jews for the
Nazis. The captured people, men,
women, and children, were held

for several days without food and water in the Paris Winter Stadium, south of the Eiffel Tower. (The Stadium does not exist anymore. It was demolished in 1959.) After five days, all the Jews were transferred to the Drancy detention camp north of Paris, and later on to Auschwitz by trains.

The role of the Paris police in this operation is undeniable.

But while according to Gestapo records, the French police had to seize over twenty thousand Jews in this operation, in the end only fourteen thousand Jews of Paris were arrested and sent to Auschwitz. It turned out that many policemen had warned Jewish families to flee ahead of time. There were a lot of policemen that endangered themselves to warn the Jews.

Seventy-seven thousand of France's Jews perished in the Holocaust, most of them sent to Auschwitz, but the majority of French Jews survived the war. French citizens hid Jews in farms and villages outside the big cities, or helped them cross the border into neutral Spain. At the end of the war, it became clear that 78% of the French Jewish population had survived the Holocaust. This is the highest number of Jews who survived the Holocaust of all the countries under German occupation. In the Netherlands, for example, only 29% of Dutch Jews survived the war. Did the French population help the Germans eliminate French Jews? History shows that besides citizens who helped the Nazis, most of the French population assisted the

Jews and did not extradite them.

And what about collaboration with the Germans in everyday life?

Paris was not a uniform city throughout the war. Alongside open cafés and clubs on the Grand Boulevards, full of German soldiers and French citizens, poor people walked in wooden shoes searching for food. I tried to show both sides.

Throughout the book, I have touched on several historical events or landmarks that serve as the story's backdrop.

Monique's fictional story about the escape with her parents describes the escape of French civilians from the German army in June 1940. The German forces outflanked Maginot Line from Belgium and were running to Paris. German fighter planes fired on refugee convoys, intensifying the disorganization on the roads and preventing the French army from sending reinforcements.

During the picnic on the Maren River, Fritz mentions the Maren's first battle in World War I. In this battle, French soldiers bravely stopped the German army approaching Paris. Six thousand soldiers were sent from Paris by taxis. All Parisian taxi drivers volunteered to drive the soldiers into battle in an endless convoy.

Thanks to them, they managed to stabilize a line against the advanced Germans, and stopped them.

During Oberst Ernest and Monique's first trip, they travel to La Coupole, a village near Dunkirk and the Belgium border. In a hidden site between the woods, the Germans built a huge bunker that would contain the V2 missiles, Hitler's revenge weapon. Towards the end of the war, these missiles would be launched against London, exploding in the city and causing destruction.

The cannon battery mentioned on the second trip to Normandy is the cannon battery near Longues Sur Mer's village on Normandy's shore.

This battery controls the areas that later would be called 'Gold Beach' and 'Omaha Beach' in the American code maps for the D-Day invasion.

Slava, the Polish soldier Monique meets at the shore, is a civilian recruit. Despite the German army's uniform image, the terrible losses at the eastern front against Russia forced the Germans to begin recruiting civilians from occupied countries, with promises of monetary reward and often with threats. Since 1943, many German army units were combined with civilian recruits under German commanders. Such companies were also stationed in Normandy, used mainly for defensive battles.

At night, Monique and Ernest slept in the town of Cabourg in a luxurious hotel near the coast. This area was also heavily protected by the Germans in preparation for an invasion from the sea.

When Ernest takes Monique to the Tuileries Gardens on a Sunday morning in the winter, they purchase paintings looted from Jewish families. The works of art were collected in the old tennis hall located on the edge of the Tuileries Gardens, near Rivoli Street, and German officers used to go there and buy paintings at ridiculous prices. After the war, some of the paintings were returned to their original owners or their surviving family members. But some of the search efforts and legal battles for looted paintings continue to this day. The signs prohibiting Jews from entering public parks and museums were hung on the gates after German occupation began in June 1940.

Although it is commonly thought that the Allies did not bomb Paris, this is not true. During the preparation for the coming invasion, the Allies began bombing all over France, with American and English bombers trying to hit railways and industrial factories that supported the German army. The first bombing described in the book, during which Monique and Ernest are in the bedroom, took place at Renault's car factories and complexes in the city's industrial area. The second bombing, in which Monique escapes the apartment and helps her neighbor, is the big bombing on April 20,

1944, in which the eighteenth arrondissement was hit.

The invasion of Normandy began on the night of June 5, 1944. During the night, three paratrooper divisions parachuted in all over Normandy, and in the morning, another six divisions stormed the heavily protected shores. American and British intelligence managed a series of deceptive moves aimed to confuse the Germans, making them believe the real invasion would take place on the coast of Calais near Belgium. During the first hours of the invasion, German intelligence couldn't decide where the American-British main effort was, so they held the German armored divisions in reserve rather than throw them into the battle at Normandy. Therefore, it was only on the afternoon of June 6 that BBC Radio began to publish credible news of the invasion's real location. All those misleading steps, aided by the French resistance disconnecting telephone lines and damaging railways, led to a long delay in German response, allowing Allied forces to establish themselves on Normandy's coastal shore. Throughout the German occupation, listening to BBC was forbidden, and the Nazis would execute anyone they caught listening to it.

The French resistance movements against the Germans contained several groups with different interests, but all had one common goal, fighting Germans. In the first years of occupation, the Communist underground was the strongest and most active among all the movements, working almost separately from the others. But as the war progressed, they began to cooperate, helping British intelligence with information and receiving instructions for actions against the Nazis, assisting in preparations for the coming invasion. The Gestapo made great efforts to infiltrate the resistance. The Gestapo headquarter was at the building at 84 Avenue Foch.

The trap, in which Monique escapes from the vehicle and Lizette is killed, took place on August 16, 1944. Thirty-five Resistance men fell into the trap of a planted Gestapo agent and were executed. This was the last significant action of the Gestapo against the underground before the battles for the city's liberation. Whoever follows the book will find that I brought the event forward by a few days.

The liberation of the city took several days. Despite Hitler's explicit instructions to raze Paris to the ground in revenge for the bombing of German cities by Allied planes, in the end Paris was not destroyed. There are several arguments as to why this is the case. The prevailing opinion is that the Commander of Paris, General Dietrich von Choltitz, chose to defy Hitler's order until it was too late, and the uprising in the city began.

The uprising in Paris began on August 18 with a general strike. The next day firefights developed between the German army and the

Resistance members who lacked weapons but managed to occupy the Paris police headquarters at Ile de la Cité. On August 24, the first American division of the Free French Army entered the city, and on August 25 General von Choltitz signed a letter of surrender, leaving Paris almost unharmed.

The citizens hurried to embrace American soldiers and turned their rage against the French women who had surrendered horizontally to the German soldiers. Tearing clothes, shaving hair, and drawing swastikas on those women's foreheads was a common punishment in the eyes of the crowd seeking revenge after four years of German occupation.

I could not be precise in all the historical details, some I changed and others I had to omit, and I'm sorry I can't let them into the story. But for me, writing this book was an exciting experience of learning about Nazi-occupied Paris, trying to imagine life in daily fear through the eyes of a seventeen-year-old Jewish girl fighting for her life.

Thank you for reading.

Alex Amit

Printed in Great Britain
by Amazon

23877843R00218